RAILED BY THE REAPER

RAILED BY THE REAPER

DALIA DAVIES

Interior illustration by Sophie Zuckerman

(@dextrose_png on twitter/@dextrose.png on instagram)

www.daliadavies.com

For anyone who needs it

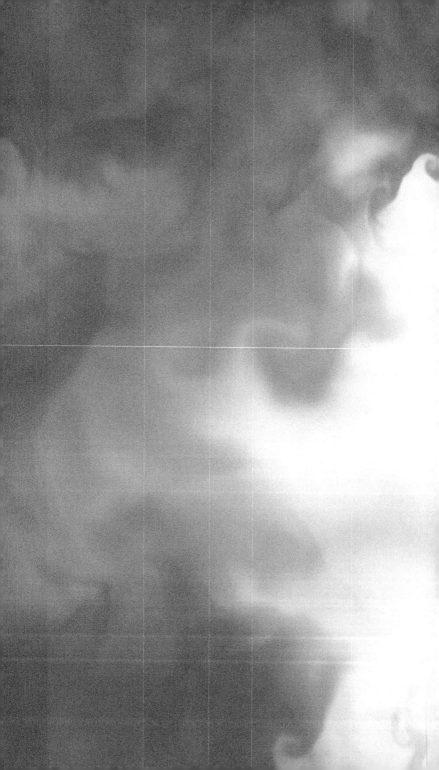

CONTENT WARNINGS

SOME ELEMENTS of this book may be triggering to readers. Please see the following list of CWs to ensure that you are comfortable reading this book before you continue.

- Death
- Choking (lite)
- Explicit Sex
- Human/Non-Human Sex
- Mentions of: Blackmail, Femicide, Suicide*
- Torture*
- Wax Play

*IF YOU'RE concerned by these, you can find a more detailed warning at the end of the book.

IF YOU OR someone you know is struggling with suicidal thoughts or mental health matters, please call or text the 988

Suicide & Crisis Lifeline to connect with a trained counselor or visit the Lifeline 988lifeline.org

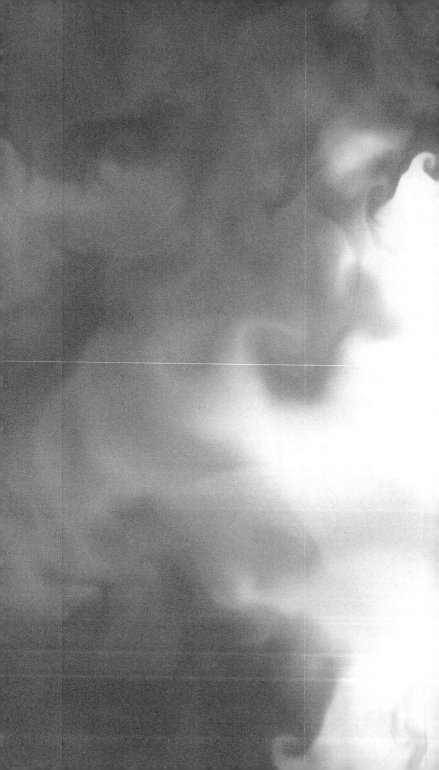

WANT TO SKIP STRAIGHT TO THE SPICY STUFF?

IF YOU'RE HERE to return to the world of the old gods, go ahead and flip through to the beginning, but if you'd like to jump straight ahead to the spicy bits... go to Ch. 4, Death's kiss.

THERE IS a secondary table of contents at the end of the book that will get you to each of the spicy scenes. It's more like a menu, if I'm honest.

I'd reccommend reading the book through chronologically first, but I'm biased.

ENJOY THIS BOOK however you want.

IT'S A LONG WAY DOWN

TO THE SACRED GROUND

WHERE THE REAPER'S

PLAYING FOR KEEPS

-ELLE KING

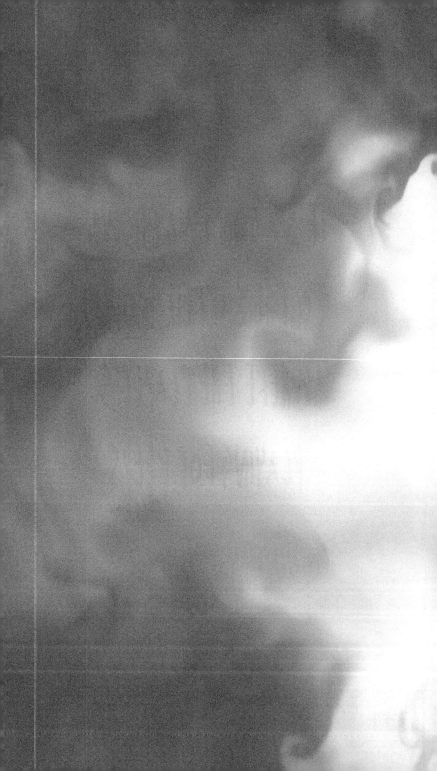

1

DON'T FEAR THE REAPER

I'M DRAWN to the dying like a moth to a flame. A moth that will never burn, no matter how close I get.

Gladys, on the other hand….

She's young. Barely ninety-two years old. But those years have finally begun to weigh on her.

I wonder what that's like.

Folding towels, I watch her through the mirror as she goes about her nightly routine.

Old women form habits.

Whisper sweet nothings to the plants, check the windows are locked, smooth the doileys on the back of the couch….

But she turns her gaze on me as she sits in her favourite chair. Her eyes are startlingly clear tonight.

"Do you know what your problem is, Onna?"

I smile down at the towel as I set it on the small stack. "I'm sure you'll tell me."

Turning back to her, I wait. The elderly lose all discretion this close to the end. They'll admit to murder, affairs, all sorts of crimes. And they love to dispense advice.

Sometimes it's useful.

"You're too old," she says, mouth screwing up in a frustrated purse. "Too old to be this damn young."

That scowl is equal parts amusement and displeasure.

Raising a single brow, I smile because the only other option is to cringe. She doesn't know how accurate she is.

She *can't*.

"Don't try to deny it. You flit around never really here, never really there, but I've known since the day you knocked on my door." Her smile is too wide for her face, her eyes a little wild. "You come and you go and always Death follows…. But he never catches you, does he?"

How to answer that question…. Certainly not with the truth.

"I can see that mind of yours ticking. You're trying to think of a way to lie to me."

She stamps her cane on the floor like it's her foot and lets out a long sigh. "You saw my grandmother out of this world, *godchild.* I'm old, but I remember the woman who appeared and disappeared just long enough to hand her off to Death. Yours is a face I was never going to forget."

That makes one of us.

I don't remember what I look like until I see myself in the mirror, and even then, it's not the face I was born with. Black hair that wouldn't hold a curl if I glued it, brown eyes so dark I seem to have no iris at all. And my skin… too many well-meaning doctors have tried to convince me I need a transfusion. But it's not anemia that makes me this pale.

"So, why are you still alive?" She glares at me. "The gods' children aren't immortal, and yet… here you are. Looking exactly like you did when I was a little girl."

What's the harm in telling her?

This is the last time she'll fall asleep. She has no time left to tell my secrets.

"No, we don't live forever."

My sister and I are the only godchildren who have found our slivers of false immortality.

But how I achieved mine is a secret I promised my mother I would keep.

Only two living mortals and two gods know exactly how I came to be this half life.

I refold the top towel, busy work for my hands as my mind reels.

My gaze catches on the black ring of bone around my wrist.

"You're old enough to know: some secrets come with a burden greater than death."

"And we both know anything you tell me will go with me to my grave."

She's right... and it's as close to a dying wish as I imagine she'll come.

"Godkin are not immortal." I look from her to the dark shadows of the corners. "But those bound to a primary god are."

"That's why he chases you...." Her brows fly high and she cackles. "The runaway bride of Death."

I smile tightly instead of telling her it's the opposite.

I'm the one chasing him.

Turning from her before that sour thought makes me scowl, I place the towels in the cupboard and take a deep breath.

"How long do I have?" She asks quietly from behind me.

When I hesitate, she says, "Please, Onna. Will it be tonight?"

"Yes." I walk the few steps that separate us and take the hand she holds out to me.

Her skin feels papery thin, but her grip is tight.

"You'll fade away in your sleep. It will be painless, and then he'll come for you."

Nodding, she squeezes my fingers. "Tea then? And one last hand of bridge before it's over?"

"Of course."

I pull her favourite tea from the cupboard—the one she told me she saves for special occasions—and shuffle the cards as the water boils.

But when her cup is empty, she looks at the clock with a sigh. "I suppose it's time."

I help her into bed as I have done every night since I arrived on her doorstep.

One last time.

I can't help her anymore.

She kisses my cheek with an ungainly buss. "You are a sweet child."

I tuck her in and smooth back her grey hair, without reminding her how ridiculous it is for *her* to call *me* a child.

"Sleep well Gladys. Perhaps one day I'll find you in the Nether."

She breathes a sleepy sigh. "Thank you for not letting me die alone."

Those words make my eyes prickle and the feel of static spreads under my skin.

That's why I'm here.

Because once, long ago, someone did die alone.

This is my penance… for a regret I'll never be rid of.

I sit in her favourite chair and open the book she won't hear the end of.

Her breathing settles as I reach the penultimate chapter. Sleep takes her first, and I dim the lights, waiting as the clock on the mantle ticks… its seconds grow longer and longer.

I know the moment she's gone.

Chill air washes over me, heralding *his* arrival.

One moment, the corner of the room is nothing but darkness and shadow, the next...

Death has come.

And Gladys' soul lifts from her, hovering like liquid black glitter. Swirling over her, as if searching for a way back in.

All the gods *choose* what they look like. Death prefers the form of an enormous black skeleton, his bones seemingly charred and brittle.

He doesn't really fit in Gladys' house.

But he's an old god.

He goes where he pleases.

In the mortal realm, he often wears a cloak of red smoke, wispy and ominous.

It scares the shit out of those who live long enough to catch a glimpse of him.

"Onna." He says my name with a bitterness that stings, and I smile in spite of it.

"I feel like you've been avoiding me."

The silence that stretches between us feels like a slap in the face.

"I go where I am needed.... And you have made certain you will never need me." A long scythe forms in his hand and he grips it with his four-fingered left hand.

The missing ring finger vibrates against my wrist.

Death is bound to me as long as I wear it... but he didn't give it to me.

This stolen bond gives me my immortality. But guarantees nothing else from him.

Anything more I have to take.

"I'm not here for you, Onna."

"Of course not. You're never here for me."

His head tips to the side and shifts, skull scraping across

Gladys' ceiling. "Give me back what is mine and your turn will come."

"No." Unlike Gladys... "I'm not ready to die."

"Everyone has to."

Despite the animosity that rolls off him like a cloud of smoke, he doesn't lie to me often.

He prefers truths. "Caring for them won't bring your brother back to you."

And there it is.

The stab to the gut that always kills those fond feelings I have for my personal god.

He uses it like a shield against me, and I *wish* I could carve that grief out of my chest and shove it down his non-existent throat.

Two hundred years ago, he took my brother's soul... and my mother took his finger.

I clutch at the bone around my wrist and glare at him. I can't tell him that's not why I do it. I can't tell him I don't want him to bring Casaran back.

He won't lie to me... and I won't lie to him either.

And he knows it.

"Take care of her," I say, looking at the fluttering glimmer of her soul.

Death doesn't say a word. His eyeless sockets are fixed on me, but he waits, motionless.

That silence wraps around me, choking me...

I have to wonder if there's anything within that charred rib cage for me. He doesn't have a heart, but still....

He holds out his scythe and Gladys floats across the room to him, swarming around the blade like a hive of bees.

"Farewell, Onna," he says, "Come find me when you're ready to accept your long-avoided fate."

He pauses as if he expects me to change my mind and then fades into nothingness, leaving only the shadows behind.

I'm alone again… even though I feel the tug of another soul not long for this world.

Death's job is never done.

And neither is mine.

Rearranging Gladys' body—placing her in a dignified pose—I close up her house as best I can, washing the last of her dishes and tidying up as I pack my small bag.

I've already scheduled a welfare call for her tomorrow.

The man in the tower isn't good at tending to the Valley's needs, but his father was and certain things still linger.

Though, I imagine Jamus hasn't gutted his mother's social programs by simply not knowing enough to care about them.

I won't be here when the woman comes to call on Gladys.

It's better that way.

I've spent too much time with the dying to know how to deal with those fully alive.

Slipping from the building where she lived, I pass by groups of people walking home from bars, evening jobs, late school sessions…. I don't enjoy how many of them look at me.

I wish—that like Death—I could choose to whom I show myself.

The mortal realm isn't my home anymore, despite the fact I am more welcome here than in Death's domain.

Maybe it's time to change that.

Snugging my bag higher on my shoulder, walk toward the tower at the centre of the city… and the tomb at its base where my body should have been laid to rest two centuries ago.

2

A BEAUTIFUL CORPSE

THE CEMETERY SPREADS AWAY from the base of the tower like a pie slice of memory and loss. It holds the bodies of the godkin and their loved ones who have passed on.

Except for the mausoleum bearing a crest with my mother's wings.

I slip through the tall gates and follow the sharply lined paths. Here, shadows ignore the moon's light, crawling wherever they please.

The steps to the tomb are clean, swept daily by one of my mother's devotees.

Inside the pearly-white edifice, three boxy stone coffins sit in a line, one for each of the Tooth Fairy's children.

All of them empty.

My brother was meant to be the beginning of a new dynasty in the Valley. Our mortal mother raised him to rule and his firstborn would have ruled after and on and on until the line was too diluted…

But something went wrong.

He died… Ari and I didn't… and this place we should all have come to rest by now… is all but abandoned.

Our crypt is nothing more than a storage facility for marble.

But this is where I'm supposed to be. Rotting in funeral clothes, sealed away from the living.

There is a statue of my mortal mother in the corner, her head bowed, her face... blank.

I can't even remember what she looks like anymore.

Our family was shattered when she disappeared. It turned to dust and ashes when Casaran...

The three statues lying on our tombs are supposed to be my siblings and I. The woman bearing my name looks nothing like me anymore. I left her in the past when this bastardised bonding broke all genetic connection to my mothers.

It's the same for my sister.

Ari fell in love with the god of winter. A god that gave her their bond... and every hint of spring and autumn drained from her skin.

She keeps threatening to fill her tomb once some nebulous future task is complete.

And then Casaran....

My sweet and cruel brother, who didn't know what to make of this world or his place in it.

The sleeping figure atop his hollow stone is smaller than he ever was, but it's the only body he has left. Not even my primary godparents know what happened to his mortal form.

I pause long enough to draw my hand along the marble likeness of his face.

I'm two hundred and thirty-five years old, and *he* is my only regret.

It's a wound that can't be healed.

I live with it.

Eventually, I'll die with it.

Acceptance is the final stage of grief, right? The point at which we admit that we will carry it with us forever, no matter what we do.

Hands on the heavy stone lid beneath my effigy's feet, I push it aside to reveal the rarely used stairs that descend past where my body should lie.

They lead to a wall of thick marble.

Marble that parts like a waterfall as soon as my fingers touch it and I step through into the old gods' realm as a shiver gnaws at my spine.

That smooth white stone continues down the tunnel for a few metres before it turns to dark slate, carved with the same markings that dance across Death's bones in the right light.

I drag my fingers along the wall, and my body remembers the only time he's let me touch him.

It remembers *too* well.

That unfulfilled longing turned to an ache that never quite leaves me.

But when the wall disappears at the sharp crack in the tunnel wall, I blow out a breath that shakes with the same tremors I feel in my chest.

The fissure opens to the one domain I have every right to…. The one domain I've let fear keep me from for too long.

My next breath ghosts from me in a chill vapour. And the one after…

I stand at this entrance to Death's domain for too long.

Courage is something that's easier claimed than undertaken.

The jagged darkness tugs at me and pushes me away at the same time. I could so easily take a step into the ash covered path and the eerie wind that I know echoes through the air beyond this rough archway.

I lean toward that darkness… but where the flesh may be willing, the spirit is weak.

I'll come right back.

That's what I tell myself as I turn away for the thousandth time, and instead follow the tunnel to the safety of debauchery.

At the end of that path, beyond a door covered in tufted, buttery-soft leather, Babel waits.

I shove through and leave the space that exists between shadow and memory.

This place… the ceiling is covered in flames, blue and red. They lick at the air above my head and reach for others as they walk past me.

Babel is never empty. Tonight, crowds sit arranged on furniture that looks as though it's made of black velvet stretched over a pale bone framework.

Everyone sees something a little different here. Ari and I worked that out the first time we came here together.

But the sign—flickering like neon—is always the same.

Babel in curving green and blue letters hovers in front of one of the walls that forever drip like wax.

Ari said hers is a steady and burning white, the tube melting the icy wall it's embedded in.

When she was here with me, her breath misted, despite the fact there was no snow in the air I could see.

The old gods' realm is full of twist and traps like that.

I shake my wrist, so the bone cuff there knocks against my skin. Reminding me I've already found my trap… I can't fall into another.

A small man in a bull mask starts toward me and makes a full one eighty as soon as he sees my face, practically running in the other direction.

Unlike the others in this realm, I don't need a mask.

Those ridiculous masks are the key to existing in the realm you don't belong in.

Unbound mortals wear masks, or they turn into horrid, twisted creatures trapped in the space between the realms until a primary god plucks them free and offers a way out.

Mortals bound to secondary gods are stuck here unless they wear a mask into the mortal world.

The rules are the rules.

But bound to Death... the only primary god who has no progeny and takes no devotees.... I can come and go as I please.

Only Ari could do the same before she was banished.

The primary gods don't bind mortals for good reason... Ari can attest to the dangers of having one of *them* fall in love with you.

Lucky me.

Unlovable and safe in all realms. Even from the Trick-ster's devotees.

It might never be empty, but Babel is quiet tonight.

I walk through the familiar space with the usual bubble of avoidance swirling around me. None of them are willing to get too close.

Devotees come and go, a constant parade of familiar masks with different bodies attached.

Most of them scurry back to the mortal realm as quickly as they can.

Most of them.

Two women in cat masks—with tails that very definitely aren't pieces of costumery—toy with a wide-eyed mortal in a hummingbird mask.

But like their patron god, they bore quickly, and their eyes flash as they turn to me.

Spines straightening, they push their current toy away and he blinks, as though the spell is broken.

I spare him only a passing glance. These women aren't dangerous, but I've always considered them something of omens... even if only one of them is a *black* cat.

They prowl to me on dangerously high heels, glasses of glowing liquid in their hands with umbrellas and flowers and spiralling straws.

"Death's wife is wandering again." Calico pretends to whisper to Minx. "Never a good sign."

And Minx responds in kind with, "Such a beautiful corpse. What a pity we aren't allowed to play with the dead."

Calico snickers before she turns to me. "Are you here to spectate this time? Or visit your godmother?"

"Or your grand-godmother?" Minx asks before putting a straw to her lips and blinking as though she's innocent in Calico's games.

"Or perhaps to spy on your godnephew for your sister?" Calico chirps a laugh. "My, my, if your family isn't fully enmeshed in this realm."

"Does anyone ever tell you why they're here?" I ask.

"Oh, lots of people do." Minx says with a nod that makes her blonde curls bob. "People *like* us. You like us too."

I do. "You amuse me."

Minx sticks out her tongue—stained by her drink—and then her gaze travels past me, surveying the others beyond me.

"When you're not mean to me."

"We tease you. There's a difference." Calico lifts her hand, tracing it down the side of my cheek... but never actually making contact. "You're untouchable... and that makes us sad."

"Why grieve the loss of something you never had?"

Eyes narrowing behind her mask, her pretty lips purse and then she leans close. "If he doesn't fuck you soon, let us take care of you."

"Maybe I will…"

Calico searches my eyes for a moment before she says, "The gods never appreciate the things they don't deserve."

I would ask if she sounds so certain because Lako doesn't appreciate them, but it's none of my business.

Calico whispers something to Minx and the blonde kitten slips away.

I let my gaze fall over the clumps of devotees.

"They're scared of you."

"I know." I don't look at her. "Why aren't you?"

"Oh, we're terrified." She smiles at me as she covers her mouth with her glass. "But caution has never outweighed curiosity for us."

No, I don't imagine it ever has.

"Do you know how many devotees Lako has?" Calico asks, her voice a quiet purr as she flicks an imaginary piece of lint from her shoulder.

"More than ten, less than one hundred?"

Chuckling, she shakes her head, dark curls brushing against her white mask. "It does vary, drastically…. But she's never had fewer than twenty-three at one time."

"Easy to get lost."

"It should be…." She catches her own tail and begins to pet it. "But there's only one of you… so, how is it that Death can't seem to keep a hold of you?"

I don't like lying, and I'm saved from having to admit the truth as Minx rejoins us, offering me a tall glass of what looks like liquid flame.

It is a question I would love the answer to… and one I dread.

I take the glass with a "thanks" and tip it back like a shot. Minx watches me with an uncertain gaze as she holds her hand out for the empty cup.

"Perhaps, tonight, I'll see what Babel has on offer." I turn away, trailing through the space between domains, and they follow at a distance they probably deem safe.

There are all sorts of displays going on, but I go to the one that has the largest gathering and sit on a deceptively comfortable sofa and lean back against the overstuffed cushion.

Mix drops onto the seat beside me, her focus seemingly on the devotees putting on a show, but her gaze is unfocused. She turns, curling her legs up under her.

"Do you think any of them really believe they'll win this silly game?" She asks, looking at the tangle that now has a few more limbs than it did when I looked away.

Minoka has set his bulls on an impossible task. The first devotee to fuck all of his other devotees without being fucked in return... gets everything their heart desires.

It's an impossible task. They can only fuck those that let them.... And invariably, the one who's closest to winning his freedom gets too distracted by a pretty new bull, forfeiting the moment they're asked to bottom.

I've seen this particular game in passing a dozen times... maybe more.

"They wear themselves out, and eventually, we all get bored." Calico drops to my other side.

Cold, sharp fingers wrap around my neck, and I still as Death dips his head close to my ear. "Is that what you are? Bored?"

The kittens don't see him.

No one ever does in Babel.

The chill of his breath washes over me, like ice dragged

23

down my skin, and my nipples pebble against my lace bra.

When I don't answer him, his grip tightens and I close my eyes at that squeeze, force myself to hold perfectly still as my mind and body *beg* for more than this single grip he ever gives me.

He touches me…

And between one breath and the next, he's gone.

When I open my eyes again, Babel is exactly as it was. Bright and bawdy, and there are two kittens staring at me.

"That is a very lovely ash necklace you have…."

The only trace he ever leaves behind.

"Is it?" I try to wash it off before I see it anymore.

It's a promise as empty as my tomb.

Again, fingertips only get close enough to tease at a touch. "I would love to see the rest of your body painted in that ash."

Calico agrees, leaning over my legs in such a way that blocks my view of the show. "I would love to know what you feel like… are you actually cold as a corpse? Or is that an illusion?"

"She *looks* warm," Minx says, but neither of them move to touch me.

"I'm not cold."

Calico's gaze drops to my lips. "Would you like to prove that?"

"What proof would a kiss be?"

I flinch at the purr that elicits from both of them.

Calico's smile shows her sharp teeth, and she runs her tongue along the bottom of that top row. "A kiss can prove a great deal of things, my dear."

I draw my finger along the underside of her chin, and her pupils blow wide. Enormous black circles ringed in vibrant gold.

She's the first person I've touched in decades who wasn't on the edge of death....

"You can kiss me, kitten."

After all, if Death doesn't want me, what point is there in wasting away for the want of him?

"Is this a trick?" Minx asks.

"Probably... but it's not one of mine."

It's Calico who leans close, her eyes tracing along my face and finally going to my lips. "If you want us to help make him jealous, all you had to do was say so."

But Calico's lips don't meet mine.

Hard arms wrap around my chest and hips and drag me backward, through the sofa and the floor... out of and through and back into both realms.

Death throws me to the ground and I skid to a stop, sinking into damp, dark soil.

Smoke curls around my shoulders like the surface of a pond.

"You do not get to play games, Onna. Kiss another living soul and I will snuff their flame."

And there are hundreds of thousands to choose from.

All around me, candles float on top of that smoke as though it truly is water. The white columns are all different heights, with flames both steady and flickering atop them.

There are so many, it is painfully bright around him and I screw my eyes shut against that light and shove myself to standing.

"You'll ignore me for hundreds of years, but the moment I decide I'm tired of waiting, you're suddenly interested in what I do?"

Death's throne sits atop the smouldering remains of a funeral pyre. It's littered with ashes held together in the vague shape of the logs they once were and coal scattered like river

25

stones. They lay beneath a riot of flowers, charred and smoking, their petals edged in golden red embers.

The smoke pouring from it is what twists and curls around my legs.

And Death settles into his darkly twisted throne. A black candle, melted into the back of the seat directly behind his skull, illuminates the intricately carved pattern in the bone.

"You may have whoever and whatever you want... *if* you unbind yourself. Until then, you are mine alone."

That's exactly what I want... but it's not actually what he's offering. He'll make me beg before he gives it to me.

He's silent, but I can feel his gaze on me even without eyes in those dark sockets.

After all this time, I should be able to read his skull and the moods that pass over his nonexistent face. But I can't.

He's kept that from me, too.

"Giving you back this finger won't get me what I want."

"What do you want?" He leans forward, maybe expecting something he could use as a bargain.

"I want what's mine."

A flicker of flesh passes over his face. Like lightning, it's there and gone almost in the same instant.

But it was long enough to see something like displeasure.

That's the only time he seems to have those flickers of emotion... when I've irritated him to the point of whatever this is.

"We belong to each other because of that little *theft*. Neither of us gets what we want unless we both do."

He knows—he has to know—that our desires are in direct opposition to each other.

One of us has to bend eventually, and it won't be me. I'll break before I give in.

Shoving my immediate response down, I stomp forward.

The loose dirt makes it more of a slosh and less of a march, and I hate that, but when I stop at the base of his pyre, glaring up at his face, illuminated by that candle, the flickering lightning flesh covers over his mouth, letting me see his mocking smile.

The argument I was going to spit at him dies in my throat.

He wants that.

He wants me to be mad and angry and…. I'm not.

But I can't let the emotion deep inside me find its way to the top.

I swallow the despair down like a hard lump in my throat and his smile falters.

He reaches his hand out and I lift from the loose soil, floating to him as though he's picked me up. Like a doll, he can toss wherever he likes.

But when I'm close enough, he draws the back of one bony finger along my cheek. "Why do you want to live forever?"

"Why do you want me to die?"

"You have to die eventually, Onna." He trails his finger down my neck and across my collarbone, leaving more ash streaks on my skin. "You time was up one hundred and forty-two years ago. And we both know that living past your time comes with its consequences."

"It doesn't have to."

"That wouldn't be fair."

"You're an old god. You don't *have* to be fair."

He wraps his fingers around my throat, and I wonder what he sees when he looks at me.

"You want what's yours… You want *me*."

"Yes." I don't say any more. I can't admit the things I would do….

"Do you think that's wise?" He squeezes again and I gasp at the pressure.

Probably not. "I don't think it matters."

And of course he stops. He shakes his head at me as he removes his hand from my throat. "You like that too much."

I do.

He shifts, seeming to get bigger as he moves, and when he settles again, I am fully seated in his hand.

He's done this before, growing larger when he wants to intimidate me... smaller when he wants to make it feel like ours is a level playing field.

But it's not.

He's an old god. He can give me everything I need... if he wants to.

And I only have one card to play against him.

Leaning down, crowding his skull close to my face, he asks. "Do you think winning this game will make you happy?"

I don't answer him. I don't think this is a game. But if it was, the only true answer is... I have no idea, but I want to find out. I hook my hands beneath his jaw and drag him to me. When I kiss his jaw, he doesn't recoil from me.

How many kisses have I stolen? How many times has he let me get this close?

Things shift around me, but I don't open my eyes to see what's happened. I *pretend* he isn't going to send me away again.

When I do open my eyes, he's back to his normally enormous size.

The form he takes that I'd called "manageable" when Ari had once asked how I thought "it would even work."

I know that my lips are black with ash. He adds yet more to my cheeks as he trails his fingers along them.

"You don't know what you're asking for, Onna."

"I think I do." And even if I don't... at this point, it's worth any risk.

Hard hand taking hold of my jaw, he's the one who kisses me this time. He pulls me to him, but my lips don't meet his teeth. My eyes are closed, but I know that the translucent blue phantom of flesh has formed between us.

When Death kisses me, on these rare occasions, a flutter of hope flickers inside me. Weaker than any flame around us now, it still burns as hot.

And like any flame it's snuffed so easily.

He draws away from me and he's done with me.

I should have known.

I should never have got my hopes up.

"How long before you'll trust that I'm not lying about this?" I ask as my feet touch the loose dirt once more.

He looks away from me. "Go back to the world of the living. There's nothing for you here unless you're willing to return what's mine."

"Bullshit."

His skull jerks back to me and the lightning flicker passes over his brows.

"You don't have to believe me," he says. "You just have to do as you're told."

With a snap of his fingers, I fly backward, and land in a field of wildflowers, staring up at the bright light of late afternoon.

I lie in the weeds for a moment, looking up at the cloudless sky, and bite my tongue so I don't scream.

That insufferable bastard will be mine, one way or another.

I'm done waiting for him to pull his skull out of his pelvis.

3

MEMENTO MORI

DEATH'S AIM IS GOOD, even if his goal is complete horseshit.

The field, with its tickling grass, sits between the city and my sister's home.

She built a sweet little cottage, tucked away into the godswood just on the edge of the thick treeline. Hidden and not all at once.

It's tiny and cluttered and the front garden is a riot of wildflowers and overgrown squash vines.

She tells me I'm ridiculous every time I point out she still has some of our grandmother's gifts.

That garden reminds me of the girl I knew before our gods changed us both.

But the woman inside is nothing like the sister I knew.

The door opens under the slightest touch, and my sister says "hello" over the sound of her sink. The water shuts off with the screech of metal that needs replacing.

Ari is pale. In this light, her hair looks ice blonde, as if all of the colour was erased from her. As if winter stole every bit of warmth she had.

It's an illusion, of course.

She hums a sad tune as she packages up a loaf of bread.

The sister I grew up with was all sunshine and spice until a sliver of the god of winter's crown found its way beneath her skin.

I don't know if any of the primary gods had bound a mortal by choice before her... but none has since.

I think Ari scares them... and they hate her for it.

I imagine all they feel for Heim is pity.

"You are staring again." She ties a twine bow on the box and looks up at me. "She's gone. And we can't bring her back."

Of course she knows the memories that flicker through my mind like shadows. We've both been alive too long to pretend to ignore each other's melancholy.

Ariadne is gone.

Gone like our mortal mother, gone like our brother... gone like Onnanaya.

Not even our godmother comes to us anymore.

Abandoned by the cruel hands of fate... I toy with the bone at my wrist. *Maybe it would be better to simply break the bond and be done with it.*

Those aren't my thoughts... I know it and even still, they dig into my mind.

I take my sister's hand, cold skin to cold skin. "Even if we could bring her back, the little girl she used to build river fortresses with isn't here anymore, either."

Ari changed twice... the day Heim bound themself to her... and the day she died.

She's broken so many of the old gods' rules, it's taught me to hope I can break some of my own.

Had I been bound to Death when she'd died, it would not have taken another god forsaking their realm to save her.

31

Death would have sided with Heim to spare her. I would have dismantled him bone by bone, remaking him until he had no choice but to let her live.

"You're falling into your melancholy again." Ari says, dragging me outside to watch the sky change colour in the dusk. She threads her fingers through mine and pulls me down to sit on the pale blue bench that looks toward the tower.

"You're one to talk."

She smiles before she drops her head to my shoulder, chuckling. "We're *old*. I suppose we're allowed to be a little melancholy now and again. But *you* need to stop living with the dying."

"Should I see if Cupid is willing to put up with me?"

She snorts this time, and I don't blame her.

It's a ridiculous thought.

Cupid would turn me around and send me right back on my way. And they'd be right to.

"If you could go back to Heim, would you?"

I expect Ariadne to laugh again, but she doesn't. She sits so still, I start to worry, and then….

"No."

The word is flat, lifeless.

I don't expect her to elaborate, but she lifts her head from my shoulder with a sigh. "Heim doesn't want me back. If they did, they would have done something more than sit on their frozen throne and pout. The gods act if they want something badly enough."

That thought settles sourly in my stomach.

"Your god, for instance." She taps my wrist, above Death's finger, never touching it. "If he truly wanted to be rid of you... and honestly wanted that finger back, he'd have found a way by now."

"He doesn't want me, either."

"Doesn't he?" She takes a long and slow breath. "I do think he thinks he can have you."

"He's an old god. He can have whatever he wants."

"But they can't. Can they?" She plucks a foxglove from the ground and brushes it over my arm. "The gods can take our bodies, but they have to earn our hearts and souls... Even Death."

"If he hasn't taken the former, what makes you think he wants the latter?"

"Your question answers itself."

I don't think I believe that leap of logic.

Death won't fuck me because he wants me to love him... utter nonsense.

But... maybe nonsense is worth a try. *Sense* certainly hasn't done the trick yet.

"I suppose it's time I start acting like a wife."

Ari glances at me and, despite what she's just said, she asks, "Are you sure you want to go to the god that took Casaran away from us?"

I take a deep breath. The memory of things I said a century ago filters through my mind. Some of them are still true. Most of them were just rage flung at the most likely target.

"Yes." And it's not a lie.

Death isn't malicious. He collects the dead. He thinks he's fair that way.

The reason doesn't matter to him. And it's been two hundred years...

It still hurts to think of Cas and what agony he must have been in to have made the deal that ended his life. But... I've done my penance. It's time to move on.

"Then, I suppose it's about time we both do something to change this lonely eternity we've found ourselves in."

She squares her shoulders and stands.

"Are *you* going to go back to Cupid?"

The god of love has hidden their nunnery well enough no one knows it still exists, but Ari knows the way back.

"I could, but there's something I have to do…. Soon, I think."

I don't like the way she looks at the tower. "Are you planning to tangle with Jamus?"

"Not in the way you think." Her smile is soft. "He won't sit atop the Valley's throne for much longer. And the woman who takes his place is going to need a little help."

I don't know how many secrets she keeps from me. "How could you possibly know that?"

"Because she fell into my lap centuries ago, and she already knew me." Ari has that strange far away look she gets when she's remembering something she probably should have forgotten by now.

But she shakes it off. "Do you want to stay here tonight?"

Ari's guest room is always open to me. I can't count the number of times she's told me to move in, instead of hopping from the dead to the dying.

"Thank you, but no. I need to figure out how to get what I want, and I can't think here."

She tips my head forward and presses a kiss to my hair. "Play this game with Death long enough and you're going to put yourself in a place to make a bargain you don't walk away from." She smiles before she turns for her door. "Or one he can't walk away from."

She leaves me there, foxglove resting on my lap and I wait until the door shuts behind her.

There are other reasons I don't stay with her anymore.

I can't eat. I can't sleep without her thinking I've died.

I'm barely alive anymore.

Perhaps someday, I'll wander deep into the godswood, break this finger and release Death from his bond and just… curl up and wait to die.

But not yet.

I follow the well-worn path from her home back into the city, slipping through the shadows like I am one myself.

One of Jamus' guards gives me a queer look when I pass him and go into the cemetery, but a car peels out of the garage and distracts him, so there are no questions to answer.

The shadows swallow me once more and I follow the path without paying any attention.

If he wanted the finger back… he wouldn't wait for me to give it back. He'd make me *want* to give it back.

Maybe it's time to make *him* want to give me what I've been after all this time.

After all, if I want to join the gods, I ought to start acting like them.

When I pass through the marble entrance to the old gods' realm, I don't follow the usual path to Babel.

For the first time, I step into that jagged crack of passage, and follow it to the one being who can give me what I want.

The path to Death's domain slopes downward and rivulets of dark smoke drip along the walls on either side of me, like tiny waterfalls.

Each step deepens the sense of dread in my stomach… but that's an effect of this place, not a foreboding of my goal. Death, despite wanting me to make him whole again, is trying to scare me away.

But that dread fades when I reach the end of the tunnel and step down into the smoky ether and the soft soil below it.

The candles closest to me bobble away, as if they're worried I might reach for them with ill-intent.

But I'm not here for the living.

Above me, batless wings flutter as I make my way through his cavernous and seemingly unending domain.

Death isn't hard to find.

The smoke—perfumed with the scents of those flowers burning around him—flows away from his throne. As long as I walk against that faint current….

Death waits for me, jaw resting on his four-fingered hand. He is as motionless as that marble effigy in my tomb.

The smouldering slope between us is enough to make me hesitate. I might not be able to die, but I can still feel pain.

"What do you want?" Death asks as I consider the thickness of my soles… and whether I would make it.

"I told you. I want what's mine."

I feel his sigh more than I hear it. "The bond is not a bargain. I owe you nothing."

"How I got you doesn't matter. You've had plenty of time to get used to the idea of me…."

"And what," he asks, "do you think you're entitled to?"

"You." I expect him to scoff or argue.

I don't expect silence.

"I'm moving in." It sounds so silly to say it out loud.

Even though he has no lungs, he moves as though he takes a deep breath. "My domain is no place for someone like you."

"Too bad."

That silence hangs heavily between us again.

"Too bad? Few would be so cavalier with Death."

"I want what I'm owed as your wife."

"Is that so?" He lifts his hand, palm toward the cavernous

ceiling and I rise with the motion, smoke trailing my legs as though it doesn't want to let me go.

He lifts me up and draws me to him over the heat of the pyre, and he holds me there, skull tipped to the side as if he's studying me.

My clothes shred to ribbons, and I flinch at the sharp tearing sound and the sudden rush of chill air.

I don't know *how* I know when his eyeless gaze returns to my face, but I do.

"And what about what I'm owed?"

Dropping me to his lap, some magic cradles me there instead of the hard lines of his bones and I feel...

"Are you trying to scare me away?" I don't look down at what his magic has formed against me.

I know what I feel.

Instead of reaching down, I rise up as much as I can and slide my hands over the back of his intricately carved skull.

"You can't scare me by giving me what I want." I pull him to me and kiss the hard line of his jaw. "If you won't let me fuck anyone else, you'd better damn well start doing it yourself."

"Do you know what you're asking for, Onna?"

"I've been celibate for centuries, waiting for you to pull your skull out of your pelvis. How much longer are you going to keep me wanting?"

His hands trail over my body, leaving ash behind... as if he's trying to cover the skin he so recently revealed. "At least one more night."

Sighing, I sit back onto his lap and clench my teeth so I don't scream. "I wonder... if this hadn't been stolen, would you have made a deal?"

"Death doesn't make deals with mortals, Onna. You know that better than anyone."

He lifts me with one hand and tosses me away... like always. But I don't land in the smoke and fall into the soft dirt beneath it.

I land on a bed covered in silk sheets, tucked into an alcove and curtained by a veil of smoke—red this time, like the cloak that wraps around him in the mortal realm.

But I'm still in his domain. He didn't send me back to the land of the living....

It's progress.

4

DEATH'S KISS

I KNOW he's there before I wake.

When my eyes flutter open to the skull resting on the pillow in front of me, I don't flinch away. I don't do anything other than yawn and stretch out my sleep-heavy muscles. I make him wait as I turn onto my back and twist, listening to my joints crack.

"What do you dream about?" He asks when I finally roll back to my side, settling my arms beneath the pillow and my cheek on the black silk.

"Nothing." I haven't dreamt since my mother wrapped this cuff around my wrist. Ari thought I'd died the first time she came to me when I slept—so still, barely breathing.

When the kittens called me a corpse, they might not have been far off.

"Have you decided how long I'm going to have to haunt you before you'll give in?"

"I will make you a bargain."

I can't stop myself from snorting. "Death doesn't make deals with mortals."

My mocking tone isn't close enough to be an impression.

"You are not a mortal." One hard finger trails down my cheek. "I will be your *husband* if you give me back what is mine."

"You are already my *husband*. No deal." I catch his hand, lacing my fingers through those hard black bones. "I'm going to haunt you until I get what I want. You know that, right?"

"Why do you want to live forever?"

A question.... Not the right one, but I'd half expected him to vanish in another puff of smoke. Like a petulant child who hasn't got what he wants.

"Maybe I don't. Maybe one day I'll give this back to you because I'm ready to leave. But that is not now. I don't believe it will be this century."

I don't know how I can tell, but he doesn't like that answer.

Lucky for both of us, he doesn't have to.

Shoving the covers aside, I pull myself up and over him, knees going to the empty space between his ribs and his pelvis.

"I'm going to kiss you, now. Is that okay?"

He doesn't answer me and, for a moment a flicker of despair licks at my heart.

This is where it ends.

Because even gods need consent.

I shove that thought away.

This is where it ends... *this time.*

His enormous hand slides up my back and his sharp fingers tangle in my hair, squeezing tight. "If you kiss me, you may get more than you bargained for."

"It won't be enough."

He moves me up until I'm straddling his ribcage and drags me down to the sharp, dark line of his teeth.

But he holds me there like he's waiting for me to pull back. Like he thinks this was all a bluff.

"May I please kiss you?"

He doesn't say yes.

He doesn't say no.

He simply pulls me down to him, but that phantom of flesh appears, translucent blue lips over his teeth.

Hard bones dig into my thighs, my breasts, and my palms as I hold tight to him. He's not soft anywhere other than those lips. The cool breeze of his domain washes over my flagrantly exposed pussy.

If I still dreamt, this is what I'd dream of.

Being with him.

Being at his mercy while he's at mine.

His tongue—I didn't know he had one—snakes from his mouth into mine. Thick enough he might as well be fucking my throat.

If I was a younger woman, I might be ashamed of the moan that escapes in the infinitesimal space between my lips and his tongue. If I wasn't starving for this taste of him, it might scare me how wet this makes me.

His fingers tighten in my hair, pulling my head back.

"My *wife*." He says it as though it's a curse. "Is this what you want of me?"

"Yes."

The word is barely a sigh and his teeth graze my throat. Sharp points like fangs snag at my pulse and I shiver when they disappear and his lips find mine again.

There are no more questions—no more curses.

He's utterly silent. I can't see his eyes, and I can't *feel* his arousal…. All I can do is take my own pleasure from this kiss and *hope* he feels even a fraction of what I do.

I pull back on a gasp when he draws his finger along my

pussy and clench on the cool air. My body wants to grab hold of that finger, to draw it inside of me, but my hands are pinned against his ribs.

"This was never going to be *just* a kiss. You know that, don't you, Onna?"

"Yes."

"I plan to make you come... is that okay?" He echoes my question in a better mockery.

"I might scream if you don't."

The flicker of flesh passes over his teeth again, revealing a sharp and wicked smile that disappears in an instant.

"You're welcome to scream. The dead won't hear you."

He keeps me there, sprawled overtop of him, dragging his knuckle back and forth along the seam of my body, teasing me.

But I don't scream. I whimper.

I'm not the fierce forest cat here to claw and claim what I want.

I'm the shy deer in the shade of the trees watching *him* stalk me. Begging—too quietly—for him to take what I desperately want to give.

When his fingertips finally dip inside of me, I can't help but angle to him

I'm greedy.

I've been left wanting for too long.

Screwing my eyes shut, I push back the fear that he's teasing me... that this will all disappear in a moment....

Rocking my hips, I try to get more of him, and, blissfully, he lets me.

A shivering breath leaves me as I work myself on his finger, taking as much as he'll give me.

"Please." I drop my head to his sternum. "Please don't make me beg."

"I thought you came to *take*, not to beg."

The challenge is there: *Fuck yourself, Onna.*

Even if I have him now, he won't give himself to me.

Pressing myself up—looking down on him with the weightiest glare I can mange—I push back onto him. He lets me and I catch a moment's glimpse of his smile.

"You look like you're enjoying yourself."

"I am." His smile appears for me again, and again, only for a moment.

"Then why make me do all the work?"

The low chuckle that elicits....

The next time I move, he presses up to meet me.

I almost want to pause and give him a participation trophy. He should be rewarded, but I don't want to stop.

I want *more*.

We work into a rhythm that is oh, so sweet, and then... I press down once more and draw in a sharp breath.

His knuckles.

He freezes and my eyelids flutter open again.

"I hurt you."

I shake my head, taking deep breaths as I do. "Nothing hurts when I'm with you."

Nothing physical anyway.

"I just wasn't expecting it."

I try to adjust my hips, but he doesn't let me move.

"I thought you planned to make me come." I stare him down and even without the semblance of flesh, I know when he's given in.

His grip loosens and slides up my side, coasting over my breasts until he reaches my throat. His grip is light and I lean into it.

"You will not hurt yourself."

Shaking my head, I fuck his finger like the cock I've never seen.

"I won't. I promise. Just give me what I want."

Each breath is harder and harder to drag into my lungs. I'm suffocating with need for him.

"Don't you want this too?" The words slip from my lips and I wish I could take them back.

It's a question I don't want the answer to, because I'm terrified that it will be "no."

But his grip tightens on my throat and he pulls me down to him, kissing me again.

He fucks me like he knows exactly how I want it, like he's reached into my mind and pulled this desire from its depths.

Maybe he has. And when he grinds a bony knuckle against my clit, I almost fall apart immediately.

"You would make such a good devotee…" He whispers the words against my cheek. "Anyone in Babel who heard those sounds would fight their way through the crowds to get a glimpse of you."

"But I'm yours alone." I repeat the words he said, knowing how true they were… how true they remain, "They'll never hear or see me."

His next words are growled in my ear. "I would cut out their tongues so they could never describe what is mine to another living soul."

He pushes me too high for too long and I come apart when his grip tightens on my throat again.

I jerk and struggle and fight that orgasm every step of the way.

When I come, it's a good thing the dead have no ears.

I slide off him, collapsing in a puddle of ecstasy and exhaustion.

Death toys with my hair for a few moments before he rises, pausing to look down on me.

"At some point, you will come to your senses and give me what is mine."

His fingers trail three dark lines down my hip and leg, and then he disappears as if he was never here in the first place.

At some point, he'll learn that's exactly what I'm trying to do.

5

A HOLE IN THE WORLD LIKE A GREAT BLACK PIT

I DON'T KNOW if Death thought to scare me away with the first orgasm I've had by someone else's fingers in centuries. If so, he failed miserably.

I feel more awake than I have in years… more alive.

I wiggle down the bed, looking for my clothes, but they're nowhere to be found.

While I'm sure I *could* walk around his domain completely naked, I don't know what other gods or creatures might pass through here.

The sheet is thin enough it only takes a few twists and knots and I've fashioned a garment that could pass for a dress… in very poor lighting.

And when I slip through the waterfall of red smoke, Death's domain spreads out before me, a sea of light begging for exploration.

I wiggle my toes in the damp soil and look for him, but he's not on his throne and he isn't lurking.

That's fine, if Death isn't going to entertain me, I'll explore his domain until I figure out how to do more than seduce him.

It's been centuries since I've tried to make anyone want me. And that was a mortal woman—mortal men had never required any work—Death is an old god. There are rules I don't understand. Rules I won't know until I break them.

There's a dark glow in the distance that draws at me. And I don't resist it.

Again, as I walk, those candles bobble away on the smoky surface. It ripples out from me like a pond, disturbed by each step.

I feel a chill weight on my shoulders. And when I look behind me, I don't see him. But I know he's there.

I search the shadows for him and even though I can't find him, I feel him.

When I turn back to my exploration, he follows.

Good.

The further I walk, the brighter it gets. There are hundreds of thousands of candles. Ghostly white pillars, some burned low, some flickering and sputtering despite being nearly three feet tall.

I know what they are—though not who—and I choose my path through them carefully. I'm not here to extinguish anyone's flame unfairly.

But it's the ones on the ceiling that catch my eye. They're a vibrant green, like algae in a pond, and they burn longer, not shorter.

"The children." Death says. "Those are bargains your mother made in good faith."

Because my mother loves all the little children of the Valley. And anyone who wants to harm them had better be ready to suffer the consequences.

Even Death.

They are high enough up, I doubt he can reach them

47

without making himself even larger than he normally chooses.

One drops as I watch them, falling into the smoke with a semblance of a splash.

I don't need to ask why. When it flips upright to float with the others, white as the rest, I know.

There is only one way for a child to lose my mother's protection.

Someone just had their wisdom teeth removed.

Green as they grow up, white as they burn down. It's rather pretty.

"Where's mine?" I ask, looking over the sea of flames.

When Death doesn't answer, I turn back to him. He points, grudgingly, to his throne.

To the black candle that sits inside the carved stone… the light behind his skull.

"Keeping me close until you can snuff me?"

He doesn't answer me.

A shame. I'd like to be able to tease him

I wander his domain and the smoke flows around me like water. Death fades in and out of view, but he's disappeared entirely by the time that smoke begins to fade. Like mist at the edge of the forest with no trees to cling to, the smoke thins and then, it disappears.

And here, where no smoke or candles float above the ground… where the soft soil turns to smooth rock… this is the source the thrumming feeling that tugged at me.

The gauzy fabric of funeral shrouds hang like a false wall. But what are they trying to keep out….?

What are they trying to keep in?

The strips are rough beneath my fingers as I part them and step through… to a place so cold, goose prickles sprout on my arms immediately.

Flat stone beneath my feet. Flat stone mere inches over my head.

The void between the rocks seems as though it was cut by a laser, and directly in front of me, a column of brightly dark light.

Why it was hidden by that veil... why it thrums at me like me like an electric pulse, I don't know. But it still draws at me.

I take a dozen steps and it remains the same distance away.

A canine sits silhouetted against that eerie flow. It scurries away as soon as it sees me and I watch it disappear behind a crag of rocks.

A dozen more steps get me nowhere closer and then... my next step places me at the edge of a pit.

That flowing column sits directly in the centre of the pit... extending down until I can't see it anymore and up....

The space overhead isn't a mirror, but it might as well be.

Pale white flames flow over the edge at my feet, falling into the pit like another waterfall. The same light on the ceiling mimics the movement.

But the thing in the middle... that flows upward.

It's not made of smoke or water or light... it's made of something I've seen too many times before to mistake... souls.

Glittering black souls.

This is the Nether.

This is where everyone I've seen to the end of their life has come.

This is where my brother and my mortal mother are.

If I could find them.... Soft hair brushes the back of my hand, and when I look down, the silhouette I'd seen before jumps away as though I might try to grab them by the loose fur at the back of their neck.

Large ears, pricked with curiosity, they watch me with wary caramel brown eyes.

Golden fur most everywhere, save for the saddle of ashy black that covers their back.

Their bushy tail is tipped with yet more black fur—as though it's been dipped in ink.

A jackal.

I've only read about the creature before, but the pictures in those books make me certain that's what they are.

They sniff at me. "What are you?"

Their voice is sharp, like a high pitched and whining bark.

"What are *you*?" Death doesn't have devotees. They aren't wearing a mask.

The laugh that escapes their clenched teeth is as dark as a dirge. "I'm his *creature*."

When they sit, knees bent, all four paws on the ground and tail wrapped around their feet, they are unmistakably that jackal. And yet….

When I walk, they follow, rising into a two-legged stance that elongates their body in ways that make no sense to my eyes or my mind.

"What is your name?"

"Lupu." They stay back from me, only getting closer when they think I'm not looking.

"Were you a mortal once, or are you one of the gods I don't know?"

They meet my eyes, unblinking. "Yes."

Serves me right for asking an "or" question.

"You were a mortal," I guess.

"I was a man and now I am an abomination."

"You're not what devotees turn into when they remove their mask."

My grandmother's oldest creature—a bent and twisted man that guards the entrance to the spire—is the only example I've seen for myself, but the stories are true.

This form is kind. Those are cruel.

"The dead need not wear masks."

I look from them to the dark well of stairs hidden by the crag of rocks they'd retreated to when they first saw me. "What's down there?"

"The catacombs."

They're not lying to me, but, "Catacombs are for bodies. Death only takes souls."

"True, but not all souls find their way into the Nether… and there has to be somewhere to put them."

"What do you mean not all souls?"

They shrug a furry shoulder and don't answer me.

Lupu doesn't stop me when I take my first step down.

The steps stop just beneath the surface, and I have to crouch to get past the entrance, but after that, the arching ceiling is high enough I couldn't reach it if I tried.

A long, spiralling path leads down, but a branch turns sharply away after a few metres and I follow it.

The new tunnel here ends at an opening shaped like an upside down heart… the entrance to a shrine.

When I step inside, the chill of the tunnel disappears, and the air glows with a faint pink haze. The floor is covered in burnt feathers….

Carvings on the wall make it clear who this place was meant for.

Why is there a shrine to Cupid in Death's domain?

There's a pool beneath that altar, filled with souls that shimmer in pinks and golds.

"Their devotees." Lupu says from behind me. "Every deal made to the gods ties you to them... even after your soul is collected."

They haven't entered the shrine, standing just on the other side of the heart-shaped doorway, they look around as though they'd like to, but they don't dare.

"There's one for every god?" I ask.

"Yes."

Then my brother isn't in the column of souls. He's down here, in the catacombs... in some gods' pool.

My mother too. But I know whose pool she resides in.

It's just a matter of finding them. Death never told me which god Casaran bargained his life to.

Lupu scurries back down the tunnel when I step out of Cupid's shrine.

"I know who you are?" They take another few steps back. "The Tooth Fairy's daughter. The one wed to Death...." They mutter something dark under their breath.

Clearly, they aren't going to be my friend.

The catacombs aren't a maze. There is only the one path with its dead end halls and shrines.

Lupu follows me like a lost little puppy, never getting quite close enough that I could touch them.

I know each time I near a shrine. They draw back, waiting for me to return to that main tunnel after my exploration of that god's small pocket of the underworld.

I find a room that smells of the Eastern sea at low tide. Bull kelp hangs from the ceiling, swaying with a current that doesn't exist. There's only one got this could belong to.

But when I look deep into the Octalyon's pool, I'm certain that my brother is not among the souls that swirl there.

It wouldn't have made sense if he was.

There are pools in the godswood he could have reached to

find the god who shapes themselves like a sea monster god if he'd truly wished, but Casaran so rarely left the tower... it had to have been a god he could summon to him, not one he had to seek out.

"What *are* you looking for? Lady Death?"

But before I can answer the question, the air shifts behind my back and, wide-eyed, Lupu bolts away.

They're cautious of me... but they're terrified of Death.

"This is no place for you, Onna."

"It is in my domain. Therefore, it is precisely the place for me."

He doesn't argue, but I know his lips would purse with a scowl if that phantom flesh moved to his mouth.

He reaches out, fingers trailing down my cheek, and then lower....

Smooth bones wrapping around my neck, he grips me just tightly enough to make me squirm.

"My domain is no place for you. But this part of it especially." He draws me to him, raising me up to meet his lips, and we melt through the stone. Back on his throne, he settles me in his lap and says. "You may explore, but only for so long."

I chuckle as I look up at him, my careless tone a lie when I ask, "Did you miss me?"

He doesn't say no, and it allows me some hope. But...

"I do not enjoy when you are elsewhere."

6

AMOR AETERNUS

LEAVING Death's domain was harder than I expected. But when I slipped out of my mausoleum and into the glaring light of a mortal realm morning, the tug to return to him was bone crushing.

I had to stop and sit on a marble bench in front of one of Krampus' descendants to catch my breath.

People were grouped around the base of the tower, putting together the trappings of a festival and I passed them as quickly as I could, wanting nothing to do with the living anymore.

It had been an exhausting trek and now that I'm at Ari's home, I wish I'd stayed in the darkness of the underworld.

The note on the table is written in blue ink on shimmery silver paper.

Helping the new Lady of the Valley. Look for me at the tower.

"Absolutely not."

I'll never set foot in the tower again if I don't have to.

I shouldn't have come.

The longer I stay here, the deeper this feeling of being two steps to the left feels.

There are many ways to get back to the old gods' realm and Death's domain. As I close her garden gate, I weigh my options.

My crypt is the closest, but I know the crowds haven't disbursed.

Gren's temple is a ruin on the other side of the city, and only cats would bother me.

Ester's spire is too far to walk to....

I should have spent more time seeking out the obscure entrances.

My quickest options are to face the crowds, or throw myself down a well. Neither is palatable, but I'd rather face normal mortals than Diyo's devotees.

A few minutes discomfort, surrounded by the living won't hurt me.

But the streets are even more crowded than I expected.

I hear whispers about the new Lady—the woman who would have been Jamus' wife has taken his throne *and* his Power as well. Not that a man whose blood was that diluted could wield the Power with any real precision.

The crowded streets only get denser as I work my way back toward the cemetery.

No one pays any attention to me. The milling strangers are tolerable, thank all the gods, and I lose myself in my own thoughts as I walk the familiar route.

Death is mine whether he accepts it yet or not.

If he doesn't like when I'm not with him, why does he want his finger back? Why does he want to send me to the

Nether where I'll never be with him again? Why does he say the things he does?

Maybe I should shove my hand through his ribs and feel around the cage to see if he has a heart I could even possibly hope to win.

When I reach that open space beneath the tower, I stop and stare. The cobbles are covered in flower petals and rabbit shaped confetti—that answers which god's line has come into the Power—and there are *so* many people.

Eyes wide, I look over those gathered.

Mere mortals make up the vast bulk of those looking up to the tower and whispering about the woman who toppled Jamus' reign. Whether or not Lily—of course that is her name —will be better or worse has yet to be decided.

I'm not sure how she could be worse. And if Ari is helping her....

But among those mere mortals I see the telltale signs of devotees out to cause mischief on their gods' behalf.

The elves are the easiest to spot, wearing their silly hats... always celebrating Christmas at the wrong time of year.

The Trickster's aren't as easy. Their "tell" is the brand on their skin. Some of them wear it with a pride ill-fitting of their god. Others keep it covered, trying to slip through the masses undiscovered.

And then, there are the kittens. My two omens sit on a wall—fully cats in this realm—watching the festivities with their tails twined together. Calico winks at me as I pass.

Whatever they're looking for, I hope they find it.

But there's a prickle on my skin... a static in the air.

It tugs at me like a sharper version of that feeling that draws me to the dying.

Panic flutters in my chest and I move without thinking.

I shove my way through the crowd, ignoring the irritated

shouts that follow after me. And at the moment the feeling eases, I break into a tiny pocket of space in the crowd.

The man standing there—a look of confusion and terror on his face—clutches his chest and I barely reach him in time to catch him before his skull hits the cobbles.

But when that fear fades from his face, it's over. His soul leaves him with a final breath.

Death appears at my side and I flinch back. The silent crowd murmurs in confusion. They can't see him.

Skull tipped to the side as if studying the dead man, he asks the question that has simmered in my mind for too long. "Do you think you're drawn to them? Or does your presence increase their risk of dying?"

Glancing at me for the barest moment, he snags the man's soul with his scythe and disappears back to his domain.

I hear the whispers start and I shove them aside, just as I shove the men in my way aside. There is no other tug, no sign that anyone else will die before I reach the mausoleum. And I keep my fists clenched tightly until I've made my way through my family crypt and back into his—*our* domain.

My anger and my question both falter on my tongue when I stop at the base of Death's pyre.

His throne is empty, but there is a sofa floating among the candles, the smoke licks at its midnight blue velvet.

"You deserve somewhere soft to sit." Death says, forming behind me.

"I happen to like your lap."

I half expect him to tell me it doesn't matter what I like, but his knuckles trail down my spine. "I cannot be soft for you, Onna. You'll learn that soon enough."

Maybe I will. Maybe I won't.

"Which is it?" I turn to look up at him. "Do I kill people just by being near them?"

"What would you do if you knew the answer?"

"I don't know."

"As long as you have a part of me, you will be drawn to the dying, as will they be drawn to you."

It doesn't answer the question… not really, but it's all the answer I'm going to get.

He considers me for a long moment. "Do you truly want to be my wife? Do you *want* to be the right hand of Death?"

"I want you. Even if it comes with consequences."

"I don't believe you."

"Then it's a good thing you don't have to." Hooking my fingers in his ribs, I drag him down to me.

That ephemeral piece of substance covers his mouth again, giving me lips to kiss.

He *can* be soft for me when he chooses.

One of his hands snakes into my hair and he grips tight— he can be hard when he chooses too.

Pulling me back, he looks down at me with a translucent blue scowl. "Do you want to be my *wife*, or my mistress, Onna?"

"Why can't I be both?"

His other arm scoops beneath my ass, pulling me against his hard bones as he lifts me and walks me to that sofa. My clothes vanish like blown smoke before he sets me on the so-soft cushions and looks down at me, skull bowed as if in prayer.

"Place your hands above your head, Onna. Hold on to the frame and spread your legs for me."

I do as he says, clutching the polished ebony wood at the top of the seat back and opening my legs as wide as I can without making my hips pop. My whole body is on display for him like this.

I wish I could see his eyes. I wish I knew exactly where he was looking.

"So obedient in this and yet, utterly defiant when I ask for something so simple."

"Nothing you ask for is simple."

He goes to his knees, hands leaving dark prints on the velvet as he places them on either side of my hips, beneath my legs.

"Touch yourself."

"What?"

"Touch yourself the way you have a hundred times before, Onna. Show me how you made yourself come with my name on your tongue and my image in your mind."

Chewing on my lower lip, I hesitate, but he doesn't ask me again.

I keep hold of the sofa with my left hand and keep my eyes on him.

When my fingers push through the tangle of short hair and pass over my clit, I gasp at the sensation. It shouldn't be that sharp yet. But he's watching me and my pussy pulses with the need to have some part of him—*any* part of him—inside me again.

The next swirl of my fingers makes me close my eyes.

It makes me want to weep.

He's right here in front of me, and I'm afraid to reach out for him.

When his hand wraps behind my head, my eyes fly wide and when he kisses me, a tear rolls down my cheek. I'm not sure if it's from joy or frustration.

He releases me and I drop back to the soft cushion, honestly expecting that to be it. I'm smart enough to have already learned that Death only gives me what he wants to… nothing more.

But this time….

He doesn't draw back from me.

He doesn't disappear into the darkness and leave me wanting.

"You wish to be the mistress of Death."

It's not a question, and he doesn't give me a chance to answer it, anyway.

Finger tracing down the front of me, he leaves a long, dark trail behind.

His skull moves back and forth, like he's tracing the shape of me. As if mortal flesh is tantalising to an old god.

"Do you know what I've wondered, Onna?" His head raises and his eyeless gaze fixes on mine.

"I've been told the old gods already know everything." We both know it's a lie. And I wish I could see his mouth to know if he's silently laughing with me.

But he doesn't give me any clue.

"Tell me."

"I've spent two centuries wondering what you taste like."

One large hand beneath my knee, he moves my leg to the side. I move the other for him, opening myself to him the way I've dreamed of doing so many nights as I lay alone in a bed that was too cold.

"One would think," he says as he draws a crooked knuckle over the dampness of my mound, "That you have no sense of self preservation."

"One would think," I counter. "That you have no idea what to do with a wife."

He laughs, and that might be more terrifying than anger.

But I said it hoping he'd prove me wrong, and when his ghostly blue tongue weaves out of his mouth, I squirm, angling my hips as if I could contort in a way to reach it.

Death makes me want the impossible. He might be able to give it to me.

"Do you want my tongue, Onna? Your body is squirming for it, but I need to know what your mind desires."

"I want you to taste me."

"Is that all?"

His thumb flicks my clit and I whimper at the sharpness of the sensation. "If you want it, you have to ask for it."

I'm too old to be foolish enough to play power games with an old god when giving in will get me what I want.

"Taste me and fuck me with your tongue, Death." I draw in a heavy breath and he waits. "I want you to fill me and take your fill."

He licks his teeth and his hands grip my thighs tightly. "If that is what my *wife* wants, who am I to deny her?"

I hold my breath, watching as he lowers his skull between my legs and all the air leaves me when his tongue sweeps over me, sizzling like an electric current.

He laughs at the sound I make, and I can't blame him. I'd laugh too if I wasn't already fighting for my life.

Tipping the sofa so that it angles me backward and pushes my hips up to him, Death's tongue trails along my inner thigh and his hand coasts up my ribs to caress my breast.

"You are delicious."

"Then why have you stopped?"

"Always in such a rush." He laps at me once before continuing. "I could make you come with a snap of my fingers. But where's the fun in that?"

I press my lips firmly closed. He's right… but I'm definitely going to ask for a demonstration later.

Bucking against the next sweep of his tongue and whimpering at the invasion that follows, I need something to occupy my mouth. Grabbing his hand from my breast, I latch onto his forefinger, grateful he doesn't taste like ash. He doesn't taste like anything at all.

But when his tongue moves, filling me even more, I forget the tiny complaint that tried to break free.

This feeling is as close to perfection as I've ever come.

His bony hand holds me down, wrapped around my ribs, one finger between my breasts.

Without that grip, I might just float away.

I move my hips against him, refusing to be a passive participant in this. I want him to remember why we're here, that I'm not giving up or giving in.

A ghost of breath passes over my pussy as he laughs at me. If he can read my thoughts when he's inside of me, he's more dangerous than I thought.

And I'm more reckless.

His teeth rake against my clit and I shoot upright, wrapping my legs around his neck and my hands around his skull.

I come apart on a cry that sends those batless wings fluttering from the craggy ceiling far above.

7

LAST MEAL

I LIKE that I've begun to expect to see him when first I wake.

I like even more that he hasn't yet let me down on that score.

This time his head rests on that pillow, and his hand rests on my hip.

"I keep waiting for you to run away screaming," he says.

I laugh and turn onto my back, letting his bones drag across my skin. He doesn't pull his hand away when I stop turning, leaving his fingers toying with that thatch of hair between my thighs.

"You're going to be waiting an eternity, then."

He leans over to me, raking his teeth across my shoulder and making me shiver. "If you wish to be my wife—not just my mistress—you'll have to fill the role completely."

I pat at the bed beside the alcove wall, looking for the shirt I remember seeing there before I fell asleep. "I'm happy to oblige. Tell me what you need."

He watches me pull it over my head and then asks, "Why do you bother with clothes while you're here?"

"You may not have eyes, but your jackal does."

"The jackal doesn't leave the Nether chamber and I see everything I want to see, Onna."

"Do you want to see me?"

"I shouldn't."

I wiggle my pants on instead of telling him he should stop saying things like that if he really wanted to be rid of me.

They give me too much hope.

But I'm too selfish to give him any clues as to how to get me to leave.

"You need to be able to *see* the dying, not just feel them." He produces a bowl with a dark metal spoon sticking out of its contents and holds it out to me.

A bowl full of…

"You want me to eat a bowl of dirt?" The dirt wriggles. "And worms?"

"If you are mine, you will have to do far worse than eat the unpalatable."

If he wants to test me, I'm not going to back down.

But I don't relish the idea of what I'm about to do.

Normal food tastes like ash. How worse could dirt be?

But even though I may not die, I have proven many times before that throwing up is still an option.

If Death wants to make me do this, he's going to get to watch if I can't keep it down.

I stare at him as I scoop the first spoonful of mud and dirt, honestly waiting—hoping—for him to tell me to stop.

But he doesn't and I take that bite…

And blink.

Pulling the spoon from my mouth. I stare at it and roll the spoonful around in my mouth. It coats my tongue with chocolaty pudding, not mud. And I crunch on cookie crumbles… not dirt.

Even the worms are sweet, gummy things that taste like apricots and peaches.

"I thought you said I'd have to eat the unpalatable." I look up at him as I take my next bite.

"I said you'd have to do worse. You assumed you wouldn't enjoy this."

Glaring at him, I finish the bowl, gladly.

"What now?"

"Now, I'm going to show you what I really am. And then, you may wish to change your mind."

The red smoke pours from his bones, falling to drape around him in a cloak. And from that cloak he draws out a red mask, holding it out to me from his dark fingers.

"We both know I don't need this." But I take it anyway.

"You'll want it."

I slide the skull shaped mask over my face and a cloak falls over my shoulders. Velvet that matches the mask, it's a solid version of the one he wears.

That scythe forms in one hand and he holds the other out for me to take.

As soon as my fingers touch his, we sink into the soft soil beneath the smoke and fall out, into the mortal world.

It's night and I don't know how many days have passed since I was last here, but the air feels warmer.

Children race through the streets, not seeing us. Green flames burn above their heads. The man who leans out his door to yell at them... the phantom of a candle hovers over his. He's not young, but he still has inches of candle before he burns out.

We're not here for him.

Death leads me through the streets, holding my hand as I look at the dozens of people still out for the evening. All of them enjoying their lives. All of them with bright candles over their heads.

We're not here for any of them.

We certainly aren't here for the woman with void dark eyes who watches us, her candle surrounded by a black cage.

"Devotees will always see us," Death says, answering my question before I have a chance to ask it.

"And the cage?"

"They are protected until their god releases them."

I nod and let him draw me through the wall of a house that looks too large next to the ones beside it.

Inside, the furnishings and fixtures scream of wealth and the man who lives within it reeks of greed.

His sharp gaze shifts as he reads through some document, his lips curling in a dark and creeping gaze.

This man is neither dead nor dying. The candle above his head is too tall for that.

"It's not his time," I say, not truly thinking about the words before they escape me.

"You have ushered the elderly into my domain for too long. You forget that the dead I collect are not always dying."

Because other gods make death deals and then they make Death deals.

Someone asked for this man's life and was willing to serve another god in return.... I've never asked what services a death collection requires. I imagine it varies between gods, but to owe a debt to Death....

"What did he do?"

Death turns his head to look down at me. "Does it matter?"

"No, but I still want to know." I want to know what he's done that would be worth going to the old gods.

Death waves his hand and one of the books behind the

man tumbles from the shelf breaking open as dozens of photos spill to the floor. I can recognise a box of blackmail disguised as literature.

The man scrabbles to pick it all up.

"He finds secrets and charges to keep them And he gives money in exchange for all sorts of things and never lets them fully pay it back."

Loan shark and blackmailer. Perhaps the bargain was worth it.

"He ruined one too many lives and one of those lives was traded for his."

"Good."

Death's head shakes. It's the tiniest of movements. As if he's surprised.

As if he's forgotten the vengeful woman who came to him those centuries ago.... The woman who might have killed him if that was possible.

Time may have passed, but that hasn't.

With a single step forward, Death's scythe sweeps in an arc in front of him, slicing the man's candle in half.

The flame snuffs as both candle and man fall to the floor with a clatter and in a heap.

Soul shimmering above his body, Death sweeps it away like so much chaff, and then, he turns to go, but I stop him.

"We shouldn't leave these here to be found by someone else."

"I don't interfere with the living."

"You just did."

His shoulders move as though he's taken a deep breath and with a snap of his fingers, the photos beneath his body catch fire.

More flames lick from his desk and a dozen books on the walls.

His computer pops and a cloud of smoke plumes out of it.

"Will that suffice?"

"Will the rest of the house catch on fire?" I don't want anyone else hurt by this man.

"No."

"Then yes. That will do."

Hand back in mine, he pulls me close to him and we sink through the floor and back into Death's domain.

Back to the cramped stone cleft that leads to the Nether.

But that is not where he takes this man's soul.

The bottom of his scythe drags along the stone floor as he walks and I follow him down into the catacombs that seem to stretch to fit him. We spiral down, further and further.

Lupu lurks in the shadows, watching us, but never getting close.

We pass dozens of offshoots and I want to bolt down each one, but I don't.

And when Death steps into a shrine where the walls are covered in a black ooze and skittering creatures with too many legs crawl across every surface...

He deposit the soul into the dark and swirling mass of this gods' pool.

"Was this the god that asked for his death?"

"No, he was once devoted to the Boogey Man, and so, this is where his soul will forever reside. Bargaining with the old gods is more than a lifelong commitment."

He made a deal with the Boogey Man and now he's here.

I look down into that pool but Casaran isn't among the souls.

I have to find the right shrine…. And I have to make sure Death doesn't realise my aim.

He'll try to stop me.

I will get my brother back, and keep I'll keep Death as well.

It won't be easy.

Maybe I'm setting myself up for failure.

Maybe all of this is folly.

I can't devote myself to another god, but perhaps I should seek out the April Fool and try anyway…. I've certainly begun to think like one of their devotees.

8

A LITTLE DEATH

DEATH WATCHES me too closely now.

Whether he's waiting for me to come to my "senses" after collecting that man's soul, or whether he wants to send me back to the mortal realm for another century or two, I can't tell.

So I give him a little more time to miss me… or to get used to me being gone.

Every devotee in Babel has a candle in a cage. Every god has a bright ring like a halo… some brighter than others.

I watch them as I sit at the horseshoe-shaped bar.

What passes for alcohol in the old gods realm are bubbly potions with all sorts of consequences. The invisible bartender decides what you drink… and you get what you deserve.

That's why I stare down at the glass that has formed beside my elbow.

The fire inside it won't burn my lips, but I don't know what I deserve anymore….

"Your lover has finally claimed you." Calico slinks up on

one side as Minx joins me with a purr on my other. "It's about damn time."

The drink that forms in Calico's hand glows pink and glitters. She tips it back, draining it in one gulp.

Braver than me.

Minx's drink comes in a dainty tea cup, but it's definitely smoking and it doesn't look... liquid.

That suspicion is confirmed when the drink she takes is a slurp that pulls the jelly-like contents into her mouth in one go.

"Are you happy yet?" Calico asks, sipping on her a second drink.

"Excuse me?"

"We haven't been around as long as you... but we know what a happy godwife looks like."

"You can't *drag* Holly and Krampus out of their bed."

"And it seems like Lily would be buried in the Easter basket if she didn't have the Valley to preside over."

"So why?" Calico turns to face me fully. "Would a godwife choose to live in the mortal world for centuries... if her god made her happy?"

Perhaps the drink she was given made her ask questions she might not have sober.

I shouldn't tell them, but, "I hated him."

Calico's eyes go wide and she sits back on the shadow of a stool that wasn't there a moment ago.

"Because he took your brother's soul for Klaus."

I flinch when she says it. I *knew* it was one of them, but knowing is not the same as *knowing*.

"Yes."

"Did he try to come after you in the mortal world?" Minx asks. "Did he beg for forgiveness?"

"Not exactly."

"The gods can be so ignorant of mortal needs." Calico snaps her teeth at a passing devotee and the bitterness in her words claws at my skin.

"How do you deal with that? It must have been lonely." Minx stares into her empty teacup.

"I don't recommend drowning or jumping off cliffs."

Both of the kittens flinch, eyes wide and tails twitching.

"I'm sorry." I take a long sip and watch as the Easter Bunny leads his Lady through Babel. The Power that simmers inside her draws at everyone in this room.

I hope she survives it.

"Did you really jump off a cliff?"

I turn back to Minx and her wide eyes have lost their lustre. Her hand is a vice around Calico's forearm.

I'd like to comfort her, but I don't lie. "Guilt and sorrow can make you do terrible things."

"Your brother's bargain wasn't your fault."

Maybe not, but it feels like it was.

Even after all this time, that grief creeps up on me like a wave, crashing over me and trying to knock me off my feet.

I tip my glass back, the fire drawing a warm trail down through my insides.

"Thank you for your stimulating company. But I think I've had enough of Babel for today."

"Come back and see us any time." Calico says, tossing my empty glass over the bar top and watching it disappear.

Minx nods. "We like you."

I don't tell them I will. I don't know if I can.

I follow the path back to Death on autopilot.

They gave me a name.

Klaus—the Krampus—is the one who bargained with Death for my brother's soul.

The Krampus' shrine in the catacombs is where I will find Casaran.

And when I do—

I freeze when I realise what the sharp prickle on my skin is.

There's someone else here.

I pause in the shadow of Death's throne, trying to hear, but all I catch are the angry tones of an ended conversation.

The person stalks past me, their face obscured by a plain black demi-mask. They don't belong to anyone… yet.

"Why do you hide in the shadows?" Death asks, looking down at me over the arm of his throne.

"I'm not hiding. I'm observing without interacting."

He chuckles and draws me up to him, placing me once more on his lap.

"What did they want?" I ask.

"They wished to devote themselves to me."

"And you didn't let them."

Something cool settles over my skin… like disapproval that's turned the air icy. "They wanted to kill with impunity, Onna. That is not what we do."

I almost disagree with him, but my mind snags on that second to last word. *We.*

We meaning him and I or we meaning….

Death has no devotees, save for one.

"What did Lupu ask for when they made their bargain?"

"They made no bargain."

"Then how are they here?"

"They are not a devotee, they are a curse."

"I don't understand."

He sweeps my hair behind my ear. "And you don't need to."

I want to argue. But I don't trust him to misinterpret my

73

curiosity. I don't want him to think about the catacombs, or their "cursed" resident either.

"I would like to go to bed." I am, actually tired for once. But still, "Will you come with me?"

Death scoops me up with one hand, somehow growing larger as he bends in half to set me on the ground. "I'll be there shortly."

I can't make him join me, so I go alone.

When I pass through that smoky curtain, it feels like the first time I've undressed myself in ages.

And when I lie down, pulling the gossamer sheets over me, I fall asleep too quickly for it to be an accident.

Maybe rest was what that invisible bartender thought I needed.

My eyes flutter closed, but Death is there instead of the empty darkness I'm used to.

Wrapped in pearls and shimmering ribbons that shift in reds and blues, he holds my candle out to me with a hand that has all five fingers. It's white and I am mortal, but his scythe is wrapped behind his own neck, resting against his spine.

One sharp tug and it would slice right through.

"I don't want it back."

It's a dream, even though I know it's impossible.

I haven't dreamt in centuries.

Death opens his ribcage and places my candle inside. It turns black when he releases it, hovering in his chest.

But dreams are just nonsense.

He comes to me and when his hands wrap around me, they feel like mortal hands. A buffer of invisible flesh separates us completely, and I recoil from it, my eyes opening on a gasp.

Death is beside me and I reach for him, grabbing his collarbone to make sure he's real.

"I'm softer in a dream."

"I don't want soft." If I wanted soft, I would have relinquished his finger long ago.

I use my grip on his collarbone to pull him to me and when I kiss him, he doesn't soften himself for me. There are no phantom lips, just teeth and bone and I don't care.

"I want you." I drop my forehead to his jaw. "I wanted you when I hated you and even before."

There is a reason my mother bound *him* to me.

She knew I wouldn't release him… no matter how much I hated him.

"Do you remember the first time I kissed you?" I ask.

"How could I forget?"

Babel had been crowded that day, but no one else could see him.

No one else wanted to.

He'd been there, in the shadows… and I watched him, letting myself believe he watched me too.

Ari had disappeared into Heim's domain, my mothers had told us not to bother them for a decade, at least.

Casaran was being Casaran and I… was bored.

I'd dared myself to go talk to him.

I'd dared myself to kiss him.

And I spent months chasing him *before* my world fell apart.

"I wanted you then." Turning over him, I hold myself upright and stare him down. "Nothing you do is going to make me stop."

"If I fuck you, will you give me back my finger?"

"No."

His hands slide over my skin and he moves me. I expect him to set me aside. He won't give me what I want unless he gets what he wants.

But he doesn't.

He angles my hips and I gasp as his fingers part me for a cock I always assumed he had... a cock I'm dying to see.

"Do you still want this, Onna?"

"Yes." *Gods, yes.*

His grip loosens, and I'm the one who completes that penetration. I shift and adjust, getting used to him, and he lets me do it, caressing my cheek with the back of his knuckles.

"Anything you ask for... that I can give—"

"Careful." I say it as a warning. "There are plenty of things you could give me that you won't. And we both know you're not a liar."

His pelvis digs into my thighs, but I don't feel it like pain. It's just a different pressure.

And then, it's not. The same eerie blue translucence that forms his cock sweeps over his hips, softening his bones for me.

I think he was wrong.

I think he's softer here in the real world. The god of my dreams can't compare.

Death is mine.

Death will always be mine.

I refuse to imagine a world in which he isn't.

"Such a possessive little mortal." Death laughs at me.

I freeze at that seeming confirmation of my earlier guess.

"Can you hear my thoughts?"

"Only when I'm inside of you, and only when you focus on something specific... and true."

"You're mine."

"As long as you have a piece of me, yes. I am."

But only so long as I do.

"And now you know why I'll never give it back."

He rolls me onto my back, pressing my knees to my

shoulders and I see the ghostly blue shimmer of his cock pressing me open.

"Other gods would punish you for keeping them."

"You've punished me for two centuries." I shiver, watching him fuck me. "You've deprived me."

"Of this?"

"Of *you*." I drop my head back, frustration tangling with need inside me. "You were all I ever wanted."

His whole hand wraps around the back of my head and he pulls me to him, kissing me until I'm delirious. Fucking me until I clench down on his cock and his collarbone snaps in my grasp.

He slows, then. "Do not hurt yourself, Onna."

But I don't want him to stop. He *can't* stop.

"Please." I hook my fingers through his ribs to hold him to me. "Please."

Please don't leave me unfulfilled.

Please don't throw me away.

Please...

I'm glad I don't finish the thought.

Even as I come apart, I know it's ridiculous to ask him to love me.

I come so hard it curls my toes and bows my back. And my grip tightens on his ribs so much it's only his godhood that keeps me from shattering more bones.

I come and come again, and Death only lets me go when I beg him for mercy.

He doesn't pull out of me, his cock just... disappears.

I'm left feeling empty... too empty.

"You didn't—"

He shakes his skull at me, arranging my body as though I'm about to be placed in my tomb. "I don't. And I never will. Is that a problem?"

He doesn't come... he'll never get his "happy ending". "Is it a problem for you?"

"No." He trails those hard fingers from my collarbone all the way down my sternum and stomach... "I find that I enjoy making you come, Onna. That is reward enough for me."

"If you don't want to do this, I'm—"

"I'm an old god. I *only* do what I want to."

9

PSYCHOPOMP & CIRCUMSTANCES
BEYOND OUR CONTROL

WHEN I WAKE up this time, I merely move from the bed to the sofa floating beneath his throne.

Tomorrow I'll search for the Krampus' shrine.

I'm too sated to even get dressed, and the velvet caresses my skin.

Why do you bother with clothes while you're here?

The incense from those burning flowers makes me drowsy and I breathe it in more deeply.

This *is* where I belong.

And one way or another, I intend to stay.

Death shifts on his throne and the oddity of it makes me sit upright. A candle comes whizzing past my ear and straight into his outstretched hand. That soft blue scowl covers his teeth again.

The candle is too tall for its mortal to be near-death. But its flame flickers and sparks.

"What is it?"

He doesn't answer. He steps down and hands me the mask again.

Someone's about to die…. Well before their time.

When I place the mask over my face, he wraps me in his red cloak and we fade back into the mortal realm.

The sea of candles are replaced with knee high grass dotted by boulders, and trees reach high up into the sky.

"I know this place."

It's a part of the godswood that is too far from the edges of the city to be crowded, but peaceful enough to draw those willing to make the trek.

Ari and I played here as little girls… at the stream just around the corner.

But it's not little girls that brought Death here. Children are untouchable…

The trio of young men, running and roughhousing their way toward us are not.

They all have candles so tall…

"They've barely lost their wisdom teeth," I whisper, even though I know they won't hear me.

"And they are still able to die."

He holds me there, arm wrapped around my waist, covered in that cloud of smoke.

I'm forced to wait and watch as they bound toward us… as a boy who's done nothing wrong in that moment leaps carelessly on a moss-covered rock and falls.

His head hits the stone behind him and the crack of his skull is so loud… the godswood goes silent.

His friends stare and then they rush to his side. He blinks up at them frantically, gurgling as they tell him they're going to go get help.

But there's no help for him now.

Their hope and fear has left him to die alone.

I grab Death's hand and wrench his grip from my waist. The boy doesn't *have* to die alone.

Pulling off the mask, I hand it to Death. I won't let that be the last face he sees.

The day feels colder as I go to his side, dropping to my knees and slipping my fingers into his. His eyes pulse wider before they fix on me and a little bit of that fear fades from his eyes.

"Shhh." I smooth back his hair, ignoring the blood on my hands. "It's okay. You won't be in pain much longer."

I would take it away from him if I could.

I repeat those soft words over and over again, praying that each time I say it will be the last.

But when it is, my heart aches in my chest.

He was just a boy, barely old enough to die and yet here he is, gone already.

His soul floats above his body, the same as Gladys had.

The same as they all do.

"Can I put it back?" I ask, closing his eyes.

"No."

My heart is caught in my throat, tears stinging at the corners of my eyes. "Can you?"

"We don't choose who lives or dies, Onna. We simply facilitate it."

I catch the scythe as he reaches for the boy's soul.

"Not this one."

"You cannot let emotion dictate how you interact with the dead. He is gone. He will not be hurt by my blade. He will not even know he has left the mortal plane."

"I'll know." Standing, I scoop the shimmering cloud of his soul into my arms and turn back. "You may collect those who deserve to die however you please. But I will not let you do the same to those who don't."

Death doesn't argue. He simply draws me back into his cloak and takes me back to his domain.

Back to the streaming column of the Nether.

The boy's soul pulls away from me, sliding into the Nether as though that's where it came from and where it wanted to be.

"I don't like that."

Death gathers me close. "You don't have to like it. This is what I am. And it is what you will have to be if you wish to remain here."

"Why can't we only take the bad and dying?"

"You are very much like your mother, aren't you? Would you save the whole world if you could?"

My mother made some dark bargain with Death aeons ago. She doesn't care about the people of this Valley. She wants to be remembered and loved... like she was before my other mother disappeared.

"Mortals are fragile." Death says, tipping my chin up so that I face him. "You know that as well as I do."

"I do. But you claim to be fair. There was nothing *fair* about that boy's death."

"It is fair because it would not matter who had slipped and fell on that rock. Good or bad, young or old, everyone faces the same consequences if they befall the same fate."

"And is it fair to make those bargains with the other gods?"

"You didn't mind reaping that man."

"I never claimed to be fair, and that doesn't answer my question."

"It is fair, because I never refuse."

"Ever?" I can't believe that.

"If this is going to be a problem..." Death's jaw closes and I know how he would end that if I let him.

"Problems always have solutions."

He lets me wander and I don't know how many hours pass as I cut paths in the sea of candles.

He follows me the entire time.

And just when I think his domain is actually unending, I find myself in front of a dark and enormous wall.

There's a shelf cut into it. A shelf that holds hundreds of candles behind a cage. The gods' devotees... separated and safe for the time being... still white.

Still destined to die.

A cluster of coloured candles sits at the back, decorated with the trappings of the gods to whom they belong. The mortals that secondary gods have bound themselves to. They burn without melting their wax.

And in among them, one that's pale blue, with no flame at all.

I know who that belongs to.

When Ari came back to life, she wasn't the same woman as before. Her flame snuffed....

"I cannot relight it." He says, without me asking.

"Can anyone?"

He pauses and I wonder if he's going to lie to me.

"Yes." He finally says, "But that is a secret for her to learn. Not one you need to know."

I'm not sure Ari would want me to know, so I don't push it.

Death isn't fair. Or Ari would be gone too.

And that means I don't have to accept that Casaran is either.

I don't have to accept that anyone's fate is set.

10

BONED

THE EERIE LIGHT of the Nether casts an odd shadow on the stairwell wall as I descend back into the catacombs looking for Casaran's soul.

I may know whose shrine I'm looking for now, but that doesn't mean I'll risk passing by any of the others.

The kittens might not have the whole story. Or they might be lying to me.

They'll say whatever their god wants them to, and Lako is as mischievous as she is beautiful.

"You came back." Lupu watches me with their tail wrapped around their feet, head bowed. "I don't think you were supposed to come back."

"Lucky for me, then, that what you think doesn't dictate what I do, isn't it?"

Their eyes narrow at me, the tip of that bushy tail twitching. "I guess it is."

As if my words predict who the next shrine belonged to, a pale green glow creeps out of the carved stone entrance and my nose wrinkles at the faint smell of mould.

The Leprechaun's shrine is filled with dead plants.

Black vines crawl along the floor like snakes, and golden coins, covered in mud tile the ground.

There is no rainbow here.

The pool of Nether glows green, as though it is filled with algae, not souls.

And my brother isn't here either.

I'm not surprised.

While I had to inspect the shrine to be sure, the Leprechaun doesn't make bargains. He places bets.

And Casaran was never one to gamble. He certainly wouldn't have gambled with his life.

This could take years.

But maybe I don't have to inspect them all.

"You've been here long enough you probably know where all of the shrines are... and who belongs where."

Lupu glares at me, suspicious. "I might."

"Would you show me where the Krampus' shrine is?"

"Is that where you think your brother is?"

"Possibly."

Their head cocks to the side and they seem to consider, but, "No."

"No, it's not where he is, or no you won't show me?"

Their tail twitches again, but they give me no answer. And if I can't expect their help... I need to keep going.

The next shrine does not belong to Krampus.

It's the one place I know my brother can't be.

If Casaran was in this pool, she would have pulled his soul out as soon as he was placed in it. And even though I shouldn't... I still believe the kittens.

My mother's shrine is something I expect others would shy away from.

It's all teeth and bones.

The walls seem plastered in them, the floors covered in a sharp and swirling mosaic. They're everywhere.

Piled high, the remnants of all the children whose lives she protected look like some tableau from a horror film.

I know Casaran isn't here without even looking for him, but what I don't feel…. "Where is my mother?"

"In her own domain?" Lupu suggests, stalking a wide circle around the pool of souls, even though I hadn't asked them.

"My *mortal* mother," I say, looking around the shrine one more time before I step back into the tunnel.

Lupu bounces backward and away from me.

"She was a devotee and yet, she's not there."

"Then maybe she's not dead." They look at me with unblinking caramel eyes. "You aren't."

No, I'm not.

My family has an odd knack for finding ways to live. If Ari and I have cheated Death, I suppose it's possible.

"If she's alive, where did she go? Why hasn't she contacted me or my sister?"

"I'm not the one who would know that."

No, they're not. "Who *are* you?"

"No one. I thought we'd been over this."

But Lupu is *someone* and I only just now realise… "Why don't you have a candle?"

There is nothing floating above their head. It should be there, caged, if they really were Death's devotee. But there is no flame, no halo, nothing to tell me *what* they are, let alone *who.*

Lupu looks away and then back again. "If you want to know that, you'll have to ask your husband… or your godmother. Whichever you think is more likely to actually tell you the truth."

But they look sharply toward the path that leads upward. "You need to go if you don't want him to figure out what you're up to."

"Why aren't you running off to *tell* him what I'm up to, if you think I think I'm doing something wrong?"

"Unlike you, I don't want to be here. And the less he remembers I am, the better."

Lupu turns tail and lops down the spiralling path away from me.

I don't trust them, but I believe them in this.

Climbing back up to the surface, I almost go back to the throne and the furniture he made for me.

But I don't know how to answer questions if he has them.

I'll have to perfect that lie if I plan to keep searching.

And I'm not ready to give up on Casaran.

The crevasse that leads back to my mausoleum appears too quickly... as though this domain knew I was looking for an exit.

I climb back up out of my tomb, closing the entrance to the old gods' realm behind me and then, hands on the stone, I take a long breath of the dusty air.

This is all the further I'll go.

I can't bring myself to walk through those doors.

What if I *am* the reason they die?

How many lives have I shortened simply by being too close?

Sweeping the dust from Ari's tomb first, and then from Casaran's, I pause, looking down at the version of myself that *has* been subject to the passing of time.

Half of my previous face is damaged... shattered. One arm has broken off, fallen to the floor in three pieces.

Nothing lasts in this realm.

"Why do you linger here?" Death asks from the shadows.

I turn to him, and step back, the marble hitting me against my lower back. There's nowhere to go. Nowhere I want to be.

"I don't belong in the mortal realm any more. You don't really want me in yours… where else should I be?"

"You know nothing of what I want."

"True." What could I possibly begin to understand of his desires?

I close my eyes and take a deep breath of that incense that always seems to shroud him, and when I open my eyes again, I'm sitting on top of my crypt.

"I want…" His fingers pinch my chin and he tips my head up, forcing me to meet his sockets. "I want you to smile."

He steps between my legs, pressing them wide and, even though I'm fully clothed, he presses into me. The fullness of that phantom cock is just as perfect as it was before.

"I want you to be happy." He leans close, whispering. "I want you to live."

"I feel alive when I'm with you." I kiss him, digging my fingers into his jaw to keep him there. "What you want will kill me."

He shakes his head and I release him.

For a moment, he's so quiet, I think he'll leave me again.

But he doesn't.

"These mortal rags are not fit for you, Onna." His finger hooks beneath my shirt, but it doesn't tear or split. "I hate the way they cage you."

"I can't walk around naked."

"No. You can't."

But Ari avoids our mausoleum at all cost and there's no one else….

Leaning back against my marble thighs, I wiggle the shirt off over my head and drop it on the floor.

His hand smoothes up my stomach, a dark line of ash covering my skin as it goes.

I watch the path of his fingers as I unhook my bra and send it to join my shirt, leaving my stomach smudged with ash.

"I have to be fair."

"No you don't. You're an old god. You don't have to do anything you don't want to."

That ghostly tongue curls around my nipple and then his teeth....

They drag sharp lines across my breast, sending tremors along my skin.

He rocks his hips, fucking me through my pants and I barely stop myself from reaching out for him

Leaning back, I grip the feet of my effigy, offering my breasts to him.

"If you want me to smile, you'll have to do more than that."

"I don't need you to smile to make you happy."

With a twist of his hand, a black candle forms in his hand. *My candle.*

I don't know how I know it so certainly. But it *is* mine.

"What's that for?" But I already know.

He tilts his hand and black wax drips onto my breast. I gasp at the pain that so quickly bleeds to pleasure.

But that wax....

"You'd spend my life so callously?"

"No matter how long your flame burns, the wax remains the same." He presses me down, onto the slab and dribbles a line of it down my stomach. "Even now, no matter how much I use, none is lost."

More splashes on my skin and I clench around him.

I have no idea what he feels from this… no idea what pleasure he finds.

He turns my face to him with a finger. "I told you before. I find my pleasure in finding yours."

"And you don't do anything you don't want to." I remind myself more than him.

"Exactly. Now, are you going to keep overthinking? Or are you going to let me enjoy myself?"

I let go of a deep breath and lick my lips. "I want you to enjoy yourself."

The next splash of wax dries red and with each scalding drop, my eyes threaten to close… my mind threatens to wander.

His teeth graze my nipple as wax dribbles onto my stomach and his magic fills me.

"They call you a beautiful corpse, *wife*. If they could see you now…."

He peels the wax away, red marks left behind on my too-pale skin.

"If they could see me now, they'd beg to take my place."

"No one is as foolish as you, Onna. No one flirts with Death like this."

He trails down my stomach with little bites, and when his palms pass my hips, my pants disappear, evaporating like smoke.

"But you're not a corpse, are you?"

I shake my head. "Not yet."

Not ever if I can help it.

Death ignores that thought if he hears it, and he draws me up, hand so tightly grasped in my hair I bend nearly backward as he fucks me and his teeth torture my sensitive skin.

It doesn't take long for my orgasm to crash over me.

My cries echo off the mausoleum walls, and his arms creak in my grip.

He only releases me when I release him, and when I'm breathing heavily, naked in the shadow of his form, atop my crypt… he kisses me, sweetly, once more.

"I want far more than you'll be willing to give me, Onna." He picks me up, cradling me against him and the floor dissolves beneath us.

11

FINAL RESTING PLACE

THE SHRINE I find first this time is empty.

No pool of souls, no decay or dead things.

All that tells me it *isn't* a random cave is the intricately carved egg on the far wall.

"The Eebie has only one devotee... a wife in name, though not in bond." Lupu says. "Not yet."

"But the current Lady of the Valley will come to rest here when it's time."

The jackal sniffs a laugh. "The current Lady of the Valley will never die. She'll leave the mortal realm one last time and then never return, but she'll never find her way down here. Her Easter Bunny loves her."

Lupu stalks away and I follow them.

They don't shy away when we reach the entrance to the next.

Folding up into that seated crouch that makes them look like a canine in truth, they twitch their nose, looking in at a literal *sea* of souls. "The Yule Cat never lacks for devotees."

Whatever might exist beneath those souls is drowning in

them. I might drown in them too if I stepped across that threshold.

Lupu and I reflect against the shimmering mass like it's a mirror.

"Why don't you have a candle?"

"I told you to ask your gods."

"I don't want to ask them. I want to hear it from you." I turn away from Lako's shrine. "I don't trust either of them to tell me the truth."

"And you think I will?"

"I don't think you care if I like you."

Their eyes narrow at me, but finally, they say, "Some of us are stuck here. There are no deals left for us to make."

But they *did* make a deal. But not with Death. Not directly anyway.

And whoever they devoted themselves to abandoned them here.

"What was your name before you came here?" I ask, letting that sliver of curious hope find its way out and over my tongue.

"I don't remember."

"What *do* you remember?"

They turn their back on me, but don't go far. "I'm not your brother, if that's what you were wondering."

"No, you're nothing like him."

That gets me a cruel chuckle.

"So why are you here?"

"I suppose you aught to know. After all, you're the reason I'm stuck like this."

That note of bitterness stings as it hits me. "I devoted myself to your mother…. far too long ago. And she dragged me from her pool, gave me back my life—or what was left of it. And then gifted me to your god. Not that he wanted or needed me."

"Why?"

"As a penance for that." They tip their nose at the bracelet. "We can give thanks to all the gods that she realised I was a mistake before she pulled any of the others from the depths of that cold pool."

If Lupu died, then they know... "What is it like in the Nether?"

"It's like nothing. There's no way to describe it. I knew I was dead. I knew there was nothing I could do about it. I was just waiting...."

"For what?"

"I don't know." They smile at me, all sharp teeth. "But it certainly wasn't this."

I look from them and then to the spiral that winds ever further downward.

"If he knew what you were after, he'd seal this place off from you." Lupu says and my heart flutters a moment before I can force myself calm.

"Don't worry." Their tail swishes as they walk down the long path to the next shrine. "He doesn't want me anywhere near him... I'll have no chance to spill your secrets."

"Somehow I don't think you would even if he would listen."

"No... I wouldn't." Their head dips low, the shadows playing tricks to make their eyes look as though they're on fire. "But.... be careful. Resurrection comes with its own set of pitfalls. Be sure your brother would want it before he's indentured to a god who cares nothing for the life he'll need to repay."

"I could ask Death to release you from your bargain."

They scowl at their reflection in the pool of souls that crawls up the walls here. "If I am not here, I am back in the pool. She can drag me out again as she pleases. It's better to be his and forgotten."

Perhaps Lupu and I are a little more alike than I thought.

12

FUNERAL RITES & WRONGS

DEATH WAKES me with a long and languid kiss.

"It's time to collect another soul." Something in the way he says it....

I'm not going to enjoy this reaping.

But I keep my mouth shut as he helps me into a long robe that settles over my shoulders like silk and floats around my feet like yet more smoke.

He's taken me with him to collect a dozen souls by now. But this one *feels* wrong.

Death's grip on my hand is lighter as he leads the way into the mortal realm, like he's willing to let me go if I want to run.

We appear in the hallway of an apartment building, the door to unit F in front of us.

It's painted a cheerful purple, but Death draws me through it and into a cute one-room apartment where a woman goes about her nightly chores dancing and singing along to music from a speaker on her kitchen counter.

And I know why Death expects me to flee.

This isn't a woman who's time is up. She isn't about to have an accident... this is the end of a bargain.

"What did she do?"

"You don't want the answer to that, Onna."

"Tell me anyway."

"Nothing." His fingers lace more tightly in mine. "She didn't do anything."

"Then why are we here?"

"A mortal man made a deal for her death."

"Why?"

"Because he was too much of a coward to kill her himself."

I recoil from him on those words.

"She refused his advances. He made a public display, and she rejected him. His embarrassment and entitlement simmered, and he went to Juun and bartered for her life."

"That's not—"

"Fair?"

"She shouldn't have to die. It's not right."

"'Right' and 'shouldn't' don't matter in this. A deal was made. It is her time."

But he doesn't move to collect her. He watches her, silently.

Because he knows this is wrong.

And despite what he says, I truly don't believe he wants to take her soul.

The deals gods make *aren't* fair by their very nature. But the deals they make between themselves are still binding. And if a god goes back on their bargain, the consequences are cataclysmic.

He *can't* let her live.

And I can't let him take her.

Not the way he's taken the others.

I take a deep breath. Hating the bargains of gods and the ways the rest of us fall into their paths.

"I'll do it."

Death's head turns to me, nearly rotating upside down in the process. "That's not how this works."

"The way it '*works*' sucks. You can't be fair, no matter how much you claim it. I concede that. We both know how well *I* understand that. But I can temper some of the cruelty the old gods dispense without remorse."

Death may not actually want me, but it's clear he needs me.

I pull the mask off once more and he says my name in that warning tone I'm already learning to ignore.

When I step into the light, I'm just a woman in a dark dress... but, even though this woman has no way of knowing what I'm here for, the moment she sees me, she lets out a sharp squeak.

Jumping back, she knocks against the counter and the mug of tea she's just finished making tumbles toward the tiles.

It stops halfway to the floor, tea flaring out from it in a frozen halo.

The clocks have all stopped too.

"Who...?" But the question dies in her throat and I know she can see Death behind me.

Her lip quivers, but she doesn't try to run. She looks at me with eyes so wide...

"Not yet." There's a plea in those two words that breaks my heart all over again. "Please."

"I'm sorry. It can't be avoided."

"But there's so much I need to do."

I turn back to look at him, wondering if we could stay this deal until she was ready.

But Death shakes his head, slowly. As if he's heard me, he says, "It is time. You have until the sun rises."

I hate the man whose name I've yet to learn.

When this is over, I'm going to find him, and I'm going to make sure his bargain is worse than death.

"What's your name?" I ask, holding my hand out to her like a scared animal.

"Rilla."

"Well, Rilla. I'm here to help you with anything you need to do in the next few hours."

When she looks sharply to where Death looms, I say, "I'll help you prepare, but I can't stop him from taking you."

"Of course not." She swallows a deep breath. "Death is never fair."

I can *feel* him bristle at her words, but I ignore him. It's good to hear someone else call him a liar.

Her gaze returns to me, brows pinched. "Why? What did I do wrong?"

"Absolutely nothing." I take her hands and she shivers, looking down at them. "What do you need to do?"

"Um…" She looks around her home and I can tell he knows it's for the last time. "Who's going to find me?"

"Your mother." I don't know how I know, but I do.

"Can I… say goodbye?" She looks at her phone on the table.

"Yes, but… be vague."

Family and friends will want to interfere and hope isn't something she needs right now.

She slips away to call her sister and her best friend, and her mother too, and I step into her kitchen, tidying up while she says goodbyes to those who don't realise it will be the last.

"This is not the way, Onna."

Death stands beside me, as if leaning against her fridge, but he doesn't touch it.

"It will be the way, if I say it is." I look up at him, dropping my head all the way back because he's too close. "You can claim to be fair. And eventually, I'll find a way to make sure you stop lying about it."

I help Rilla move through the apartment. Turning off the kettle so that it won't set her apartment on fire and cause even more death. Disposing of the embarrassing items she wouldn't want her mother to find when she cleans out the remnants of Rilla's life....

I stop her before she pulls the vacuum out. "The dust doesn't matter."

"Maybe I'm stalling." She offers me a weak smile. "I asked my mother to come by tomorrow. So I don't go too long without being found."

For the other tenants.

Everything she's done was meant to keep others from being burdened by her death.

When she goes to her bedroom, I follow, and Death trails in both our wakes. She glances back at us as she slips into the bathroom.

"I don't want to embarrass them when they find me."

I help her change into her pyjamas and slide into her bed.

It's a task I've performed hundreds of times. But the elderly have lived lives they can leave behind. Rilla didn't get the chance.

"I promise you, this will be painless.... But I will make sure he suffers for what he's done."

"He?" There's a recognition in her eyes that I hate.

"You didn't do anything wrong," I say again.

I hold out my hand and Death steps out of that shadow that follows him everywhere. Rilla looks up at him with eyes so wide I don't know if they'll ever close again on their own.

But Death doesn't reach out for her with his scythe, he holds out one of his long, bony hands.

She glances at me once more, and a tear rolls down her cheek as she takes his hand. The moment their fingers touch, her soul leaves her and I catch her body before it falls, laying her gently back on her pillows, arranging her so she looks as though she passed in her sleep.

Her spirit floats in Death's hand as he waits for me.

"I do not decide who lives or dies, Onna. That is how I am fair."

I take her from him. "We will have to continue to disagree on what that word means."

13

BE THE CHANGE YOU WANT TO SEE IN THE UNDERWORLD

RILLA SLIPS FROM MY FINGERS, swirling up into the Nether as though caught on a tiny cyclone.

"All mortals die," Death says, quietly, his skull tipped down to look at me, but I can't meet his sockets.

I wonder how long my flame would have burned without interference.

I stare at the flowing Nether, hating it.

There was a time I thought those souls that found their way to this place were at peace. But what Lupu told me... the sense of *waiting*.

"Her time would have come—"

I shake my head. "I don't want to hear it."

I don't want to talk about the fact that we all have to die. I don't want to be here.

I need space and I need to just not be around him until I figure out what needs to happen moving forward.

Turning on my heel, I stalk out of Death's domain.

And he doesn't stop me when I go.

I wander into Babel, mindlessly. It feels like the only place I can go... even with its innumerable wandering eyes.

The mortal realm feels like it would only make me destructive.

My mother's domain is full of teeth and turmoil and I want peace... but not the kind I'd find in my grandmother's.

Butterflies and bluebells and tulips mixed with daffodils... Ester's domain is not the escape I need right now.

I don't want cheerful pinks and sighing breezes.

There is an ache in my chest I haven't felt for a century. Grief never leaves... it just buries itself until something brushes that covering away.

I want the Earth to devour me whole and absorb me.

It's a hollow and sucking pain that makes me want to break myself apart. A dull familiar anger that makes me want to break someone else into a dozen pieces.

I won't try to explain myself to my grandmother. She is crueller than most of the old gods... no matter how sweet she may seem.

She would see nothing unjust in that woman's death.

She would have made the deal that killed Rilla if that man had brought his bargain to her. She creates life with the intention that it *will* die.

She *likes* that things die.

I still don't know exactly how the lines split when the primary gods fought over my sister's life. I don't know which of them would have let her pass into the Nether, simply for loving Heim... but there's a cold and slithering dread in the pit of my stomach that tells me Ester was not the god who took Heim's side.

One of my grandparents *wanted* her to die.

I need the space to think and I need to make up my mind. I can't do that with Death watching. But there are few places he won't see me.

Fewer still where I'm welcome.

Babel feels a little quieter this time.

Hushed voices from dark corners, not moans or screams.

The kittens appear out of nowhere, like the omens I've always thought they were.

"My, my!" Calico smiles at me with her sharp, white teeth before her eyes dart away from me, narrowing at those dark places and the people hidden in them. "Look how they skitter away. They know how dangerous you are."

"Why should they run? It's not like I can do anything to them."

"That's not quite true, though." Minx purrs on my other side, the soft fur of her tail brushing against my leg. "Is it?"

"I'm not in the mood for your games today."

"That's fine, we were asked to collect you." Calico slips her fingers in mine and I flinch as she squeezes my hand.

"That *is* dangerous."

"We know better than to toy with you now that you've actually claimed him." Calico's laughter drowns out her purr as Minx takes my other hand and they keep me close, between them.

A few metres later, they link arms with me and pull me in tight, as though we're squeezing through some opening that's far smaller than the expanse of Babel around us.

When Minx lays her head on my shoulder, a ridiculous thought flutters through my mind and out of my mouth before I can stop it. "Are you trying to cuddle?"

"You're not in a good place right now," Minx says, hugging my arm. "We want you to know you're loved."

Calico knocks her cheek against mine, and I hear the low rumble of a purr inside her. "The old gods' realm tends to make people forget that when they're here long enough."

"You two have been here far longer than any other devotee I've met... how have you survived this long?"

"We have each other, silly."

They look over me, to look at each other.

I haven't seen many people in love and *believed* it. But these two women love each other more than even their god probably realises.

But they *found* love in this realm and they've held onto it for…. ever.

"Oh, sweet, sweet, corpse. Wipe that look off your face right now." Minx's nail digs into my cheek as she forces me to meet her eyes.

It's so sharp and she's so soft that I freeze, blinking at her.

"Whatever you think you know about us. You don't. Whatever you think knowing about us means to you… it doesn't."

Chuckling as she slips Minx's hand away from my face, Calico says, "What my favourite creature in all the realms is trying to say is, worry about yourself right now, Onna. This isn't our story. Your questions don't have our answers."

They draw away from me, eyes going to the narrow space in a doorway crammed full of antlers.

"Gren is waiting for you, sweet corpse."

"Go in, or don't. That's up to you, we've done our job."

They blow me a kiss in a synchronised pucker of their lips and then disappear into the shadows.

I'm one of a very few that has the option to ignore an old god's summons. Perhaps the only one who can ignore a primary god's. But curiosity is a tug I can't ignore, and I'm in a self destructive mood.

What better way to feed that need than by going to an old god whose favourite pastime is arguing until someone—or something—breaks.

I take a deep breath. Of my grandparents, Gren is the less

cruel of the two.... Though they can be ruthless if they want to.

The antlers scrape at my skin, slicing my flesh... but I don't bleed.

The wounds heal almost as quickly as they appeared.

I wonder... if I give back Death's finger, would those marks reopen? Would every wound I've endured without ever wearing it on my skin reappear?

It's a pointless thought exercise.

I'm not giving the finger back.

I'll never know.

I walk through piles of leaves that cover the floor of Gren's domain in a crunch layer up to my knees.

Slogging through them like freshly powdered snow. I make my way to the centre of Gren's domain. To the ridiculous space that looks like the interior of a massive tree that's been hollowed out.... If a tree was kilometres wide at its base.

The pinprick of light far above shines down like a spotlight on the centre of the pool and the mangled root-ball of a throne there.

But Gren isn't here.

It's a power move they don't need to exercise, and yet...

Their throne is empty and I bat away the leaves that fall, not letting them touch me for long enough to change into whatever trick the god of autumn wants to play.

There's nothing in front of their throne. Nowhere to sit and wait, and I'm too tired to stand after Rilla's reaping.

There's an ache in my bones... a weariness that makes me feel my age.

And there's a swing I remember from when I was a little girl.

It hangs from a tree near that mirror glass pool. Some things don't change as quickly as others.

It creaks as I sit, but it still holds my weight and I sway a little, as if pushed by nonexistent wind.

But sitting still only lets my mind wander and the word "fair" skitters through my mind like a creature with spindled legs tipped in claws, and fangs that slice.

Ivy curls its way up my legs and I let it as the first tear rolls down my cheek.

I wonder how long it would take for Death to come looking for me if I let it consume me. If I stayed here as a living topiary until this empty feeling left my chest.

But that was never going to be an option.

One moment I'm alone with those tears, and the next, Gren is behind me, their chin resting on my shoulder. "Stop feeling sorry for yourself."

They draw away and the antler-like crown that keeps their dark hair a mess pulls my hair with them, like fingers tangling in the strands.

Today, they wear the legs of a dear and have wooden hands. Their teeth are sharp and their eyes flat discs of opal.

Gren is rarely the same god for long.

"It's high time you start acting like Death's bride and change the rules."

"Did you bring me here to scold me?"

Their opal stare turns on me, but they don't say the things I imagine their irritation would like them to.

"He does not want to change."

"The bond may have broken the connection you and I have, but my daughter is still your mother. There may be none of her left in your blood, but the bonds don't change a person's soul."

When I don't say anything, they scrutinise me. "You think we're cruel and unfair?"

I look at them, wondering if they truly want an answer.

"Death doesn't *need* to be. He chooses to because he has no reason to change and no one to show him how."

"She shouldn't have had to die."

"I agree. But even so, why should she have to languish in that river of souls? Why should she have the same end her killer will eventually find as well?" They draw a cold, wet finger along my cheek. "Do you know why you're drawn to the dying, child? It's because you have *his* power. A godchild bound to a primary... you could so easily destroy the world if you wished it."

"I can't do what Cassaran did... I may be godborn, but we both know I never had the Power."

"You don't need Ester's Power. You have your own." They shake their head at me, the dangling moss swaying from their antlers. "Our connection was broken when your mother bound him to you... but it was replaced. You are joined. What is his, is yours."

They sigh, letting go of me and swirl away from me as though the water lapping at their hooves pulls them in the flow.

"Death has so many favours piled up throughout the years. Perhaps you should be the one to call them due. He needs shaking up, so finish what you started. Claim your place and your power... and create the justice you say you want."

"Knowing when others will die doesn't help me. I can't stop him from taking them."

"You don't have all of his power, of course, but enough to get yourself in trouble.... Enough to do the things he's too stagnant to do." The looming shadow I've always thought was their true form blocks out the pinprick of light overhead. "The Power that Ester gives is different, yes. But you don't need to change the mortal realm."

"I can change his domain?"

"He can make his domain into anything he wishes and the power there…. It affects the dead in ways I'm not sure even I can imagine."

I can change his domain….

"Force the change you want, Onna. Or the one you don't may find its way into being."

Gren sweeps their hands at me like they're shooing me away and I land flat on my ass in the middle of Babel, still tangled in ivy.

14

SUFFERING & BLISS

I CAN STILL HEAR the kittens snickering at me as I step back into Death's domain. They had a front-row seat to my graceless return to Babel, but I didn't let them get much of a look.

Gren is right.

Death is mine… if I can use their power, even a little bit of it, then I have to try.

Thankfully, he isn't on his throne when I return.

Death's domain is empty.

I don't see him as I hurry through the sea of candles like a child about to do something they hope their parents won't catch them at. The smoke swirls a path behind me, candles bobbling in my wake.

I'm not sure if he's giving me space, or if he's collecting another soul, but it's for the best that he's gone.

He isn't waiting for me when I reach the Nether.

Lupu is. But the jackal isn't going to interfere with my plans.

"I don't like the look on your face…." Lupu jumps back from me, tail low and twitching. "What are you going to do?"

"I think it's time we change Death's definition of 'fair', don't you?"

I don't look at them, but I hear the sniff of disagreement.

"I don't think anything. Don't drag me into it."

"Oh, don't worry. He won't have anyone to blame but me… and maybe himself."

The Nether swirls and flows upward, unchanged, and the empty space around it feels too big. Or maybe I feel too small for what I'm about to do.

I glance at the bone around my wrist as I go to my knees, placing my hands on the hard cool ground that feels like slate.

Cassaran could do anything he thought of with the snap of his fingers or a clap of his hand. But he hadn't needed the physical signal, it had simply helped him focus.

Rilla and Gladys and Cassaran and the boy who fell…. They don't deserve to be in the same soul soup as loan sharks and crooked landlords. Separating them required more than just desire, it meant putting them some place they were worthy of the eternity they faced.

I held those two ideas in my mind. Dragging the purest forms of each that I could think of and then I called on every last bit of will inside me. Every thread of strength that held me together.

Squeezing my eyes shut, I grit my teeth against the pain of it, against the burning coil of the bone around my wrist.

And then, like a bubble, the pain and the pressure and the screaming chime in my ears… they burst and I sag to the ground.

Face pressed against the floor, energy seeps out of me like blood flowing from an open wound. Every part of my body aches, my vision is hazy and… the hair that has freed itself to fall in front of my face is snow white.

I honestly wouldn't be surprised if all of the colour has leached from me.

I use what strength I can find and shove myself over, rolling until I'm on my back and I look up at what I've created….

A long stone bridge juts out over the pit, cutting through the Nether that flows around it. And at its end a pair of archways. Two shimmering doorways. Two gilded gates…

Suffering and Bliss.

Maybe some deserve nothing… but others deserve these.

Death stands beside me and for once, I'm glad he has no face to show his emotions.

I don't want to know if he's mad.

I don't want to know if he thinks I'm a fool.

He doesn't have to be just, but I'll make him change his definition of fair.

"Which did you create for me?" He asks. No censure or irritation in his voice, but I'm too tired to answer him.

"Lupu," I say, looking up at the jackal. "Will you help me up?"

They look briefly at Death, their eyes wide, but they come to me, paws out and help me to my feet.

But they only help me to standing and then skitter away.

It's Death who keeps me upright. His touch pushing energy back into me, but I yank my arm away from him when I have just enough to manage on my own.

I take my first step onto the bridge and the sharp stone floor hits harder against my bones. I ignore it. There are more important things to do right now.

The bridge splits the Nether in two and wind whips at me as I cross into the divide I've created.

It's so quiet here… like the Nether eats all of the sound

around me, but I can *feel* the souls coiling and curling and flying around me. There is no rest in this cascading chaos.

It buffets me as I make my way to the very centre of that great black pit, but when I reach out, it doesn't recoil from me. And I draw on Death's power once more.

Dipping my fingers into the stream, I think Rilla's name… and catch her soul a moment later.

She slips between my fingers and into my palm, like a snake, coiling into my grasp. Phantom hands claw at me, trying to catch hold and be pulled free, but I only have one more soul I can take at the moment.

I don't need to know the boy's name. He slips into my palm a moment later, too. And I draw them out of the swirling miasma, holding them close as I make my way across to the doorways that float just beyond the stream of the Nether.

And when I pass both of them through, some of the weight I've carried for too long goes with them.

One by one, I pull those that I know deserve Bliss from the Nether and ferry them to their rightful end.

The odious loan shark catches at my hand when I'm searching for Gladys. It's his turn to suffer.

Death stands at the end of the bridge, watching.

"Sorting through them will take a lifetime, Onna." He reaches for me and draws me back to him.

"I don't care." I try to move around him, but he doesn't let me.

Lupu is gone and I have a feeling if I had any sense left, I should probably be scared of what Death has in mind for me right now.

I've stolen from him, again… and I don't feel in the mood to apologise.

When he lifts me off the ground, I can feel the energy I'd lost coursing back into me.

"You should not have done that, *wife*."

"Why not?"

"Because the equality of death is a constant."

"The *equality* of death wasn't ever fair and I refuse to let it continue."

"If one woman's death causes you to change the structure of our world, you were not meant to share in this place with me. My job is simple. Complicating it will only cause problems."

I'm not the one to pass judgement on these souls. That's true. I don't understand them and I can't know what they deserve…. But I can figure it out.

It's going to take time. But I have plenty of that… "I'll work my way through them, for as many lifetimes as it takes."

"This is folly."

"I guess we'll just have to see."

I wriggle out of his arms and he lets me go.

There's one more thing I have to do before I can come back to sort the rest of the souls.

15

A CRUEL CRUEL SUMMER

FROM THE DARK and heady smoke of Babel to the glaring white heat of Juun's domain, I trail an ashen line behind me.

The summer god scowls at it when I step up onto the floating terrace. Her gaze barely leaves the dark line as I weave through clusters of cat-shaped cacti and metal snakes that slither away from me… even as they coil to strike. Juun sits on her throne made of men. Bare and bleeding, they're bound in barbed wire. She waits for me as though she expected me.

Her hair lays flat on her head as if it's been glued down. The glassy smooth strands are twisted into flat curls and waves that flicker like fire and water all at once.

She doesn't speak.

Her hands are curled, long nails digging into the arms of the men who form the sides of her throne, and she watches me with sharp and greedy eyes.

Keeping a god curious is one of the few ways to maintain the upper hand.

It is possibly the only way available to *me*.

Her head tilts as I near, one brow rising sharply, as if she can't quite decide what she thinks of me.

If I wasn't used to the old gods, she might have scared me. But they're more pompous than they deserve. And as long as Death's finger is firmly around my wrist, her cruelty can't reach me.

It's that knowledge that she can't touch me that lets me step closer to her than I ought. Her smile is amused as she trails her gaze over me one last time before she says, "My, my. You are as lifeless as the whispers say."

I don't tell her the change is recent.

"Rid yourself of that cloak and you could bury yourself in my sand, never to be seen again."

"Perhaps another time."

Her lips twitch in irritation. "I did not realise binding Death meant you relinquished your sense of humour."

"I'm in no mood to laugh."

"No, I don't imagine you would be... forced to live with the dead as you are."

One of the men beneath her groans, and she twists, shifting her weight and twisting the wires, cutting into all of the men supporting her. Her hissed command for quiet snaps across the terrace and the whimper dies immediately.

She looks too pleased when she turns back to me.

"You're here for something. Out with it, girl." She keeps her eyes on me, but movement draws mine down to the ground at her feet. One of her shoes grows as a wickedly spiked heel. She uses it to stab straight through one of her throne's hands and into the stone beneath it.

He grits his teeth as the blood wells and flows onto the stone beneath his palm.

Given what I know of the bargains she makes, I refuse to feel sorry for him.

"A man came to you and bargained for a woman named Rilla's life."

She smiles, her teeth longer and sharper than they were a moment before. "And you collected it for me. That was very kind of you."

"Kindness had nothing to do with it. I want to see him."

"Do you?" Lifting her foot out of the man's hand, she places it back onto the clean stone in front of her and that heel shrinks until it disappears and her foot lays flat. "Why would you want to do that?"

"I think you'll enjoy the result if you take me to him."

She hums, leaning back and reaching up to scratch long lines from the neck of a man behind her.

His eyes flutter and he sways and for a moment I think he might pass out.

But he flinches and stays rigidly upright as the dark and spindly branches of a cactus that look dead grow and press closer behind him.

"If I take you to him, will you tell me what that great and terrible rumble was from Death's dark domain?"

"No."

That makes her smile and I wait.

Finally, she stands, using the motion and her weight to throw the throne to the hard ground, and I look away as skin snags on metal and spines.

"I was growing bored, anyway."

Trailing in her wake, I stay clear of the cactus clumps and the skittering scorpions that seem to infest her domain.

She leads me off of her terrace and into the sand, past dozens of devotees in various stages of pain.

When we finally stop, It's in front of a man who is held to a metal post by a coil of concertina wire lined with rusted razors.

His skin is red and blistered, his lips are chapped and his jaw moves as if asking for water, though he doesn't make a sound.

"What did he offer in exchange for Rilla's life?"

"What most men offer me thinking I'll use it in a way that benefits them." She smiles up at him, her teeth sharp like fangs and he flinches back, crying out when the blades dig into him.

"They always offer me their bodies, never once considering the joy I take in breaking my toys."

Hands clasped behind her back, she watches him as if he is a piece of art.

"How long is his sentence?"

"He didn't specify a duration... more the fool him."

"Good." I pull on Death's magic again, twisting my hand as I close it in a fist, and the wires cinch tight, blades digging into his tortured skin.

Juun's eyes glitter with a dark fire as she turns from him to me.

"Promise me he'll never leave this realm." I don't want him in my domain, even if he spends the rest of eternity suffering. He can do that here.

"If he does ever serve out his sentence," she says, gaze tracing over the dark lines of blood running down his skin. "I can assure you the man he is now is not the man he will be."

I suppose it's the best I can ask for. The gods do not do favours freely and I have too little to bargain with... or do I?

"What did Death ask for to complete this man's bargain."

"He has yet to inform me." She smiles and I know she thinks she has nothing he needs.

"Then I will finish this bargain for him. As his wife, it is my right."

"Oh…" Her smile is wide and wild. "I think I'm going to like this."

"He never leaves." I meet the man's terrified eyes. "He will live forever. Here. And his pain will be unending."

"As you wish."

"Death is too kind for men like him." With one last squeeze of my fist I turn back for Babel, and Juun keeps pace.

She walks with me as though we're friends.

"I think I like you, little corpse." She chuckles and her laughter sounds like crackling embers. "You certainly have more spine than either of your siblings."

"Is that why you wanted Ari to die? Because she didn't have a strong enough spine?"

"No. I wanted her to die because she made Heim happy and he doesn't deserve it."

"Were you jealous?"

She laughs, but she doesn't deny it and when I reach the edge of her domain, she says, "Come visit me anytime you wish to help punish my devotees."

16

HEADS WILL ROLL

DEATH WAITS for me on his throne once more, chin resting in his palm. "Did you find what you were looking for?"

I don't answer that. I won't let him bait me. I'm already mad enough as it is.

This time, I don't hesitate to climb the smouldering mound, letting coals and soil fall into the smoke and sizzle. The burning flowers crumble to ash as soon as my cloak brushes against them.

I want to stamp them all out. I want to shove the ashes and coals away until his throne is down in the smoke. Maybe then he'll be less of an aloof asshole.

Death doesn't do anything to help me as I climb up his throne to stand on it, between his legs. If he had a real cock, I'd have my foot on it now. But there's nothing I can do to make him uncomfortable. Nothing I can do to let him *feel* how angry I still am.

"There has to be a better way." I refuse to believe that I have to sit back and just *let* the old gods kill whomever they choose.

"I could have lifted you up if you asked," he says, wilfully misunderstanding me.

"That's not what I meant, and you know it."

"Do I?" He wraps one hand around me and lifts me up so that I am eye level with him. He's not as big as I've seen him before... but he's still too big for me to do it on my own.

I don't like the unsteady feeling I get as my feet dangle, so I place them between his ribs, using them to steady myself.

"Your definition of fair is flawed. And I won't allow you to be complicit in murder anymore." I glare at his sockets, fists clenched and nails digging into my palms so I don't scratch at his bones. "From now on, you will consult me before you make any other deals."

He's so still, I could imagine he was a statue, and then, finally... "I won't agree to that."

He *won't* agree to it. Not he *can't*.... Not he *shouldn't*.... He won't.

I'm not certain what comes over me, but I grab hold of his skull. Using my foothold on his ribs for leverage, I twist and yank.

I wrench his head free and throw it, as hard as I can, away from me.

But it doesn't fall to the ground in a crash of dirt and a swirl of smoke.

Death reaches out his hand and the tumbling skull freezes in mid air before it comes back to us as though on a retractable cord.

"That wasn't very nice." He says as he places it back on his cervical vertebrae and clicks it into place.

"I didn't feel like being nice."

"Perhaps I don't either."

Dark cords like shadow snap out to catch my wrist and they lift me off the floor, dangling me like a marionette. They wrap around me shoving beneath the cloak he gave me and pulling it away as they wrap me up tight, fondling me and prodding me.

More still snap around my ankles, pulling them up, opening me as they draw me toward him and his ghostly tongue snakes out of his teeth.

It slides over me, barely slipping into me… but it's enough.

I exhale and the breath leaves me like a whimper… like a flutter of wings trapped inside my lungs.

It slithers and snakes into me.

Never far enough.

Death teases me and I press my lips together, refusing to beg.

I'm mad at him.

I'm *furious*. But I want this. I always want him.

One hand beneath me, holding me like a seat, he lifts me to his mouth. This time, his whole face appears in that blue translucence.

Brow's knit, he glares at me, still without eyes and seals his ghostly lips to me, sucking my clit so hard, I scream.

"Disobedience should be punished."

If this is how he plans to punish me, I'll find every way to disobey.

"But you've already punished yourself enough, haven't you?"

When he pulls away, I make a sound that makes me flinch away from myself, it's so inhuman.

He turns me into a creature of need.

"I should be mad at you for taking my power."

"But you're just disappointed?" I wriggle my hips, trying to get to him.

"I assume Gren is the one who told you you could use it."

"I always know where you are, Onna. I'm always with you. You are my greatest distraction and the only being in any of the realms I care for." Something like lightning cracks over his phantom face before it disappears. "I am mad at you because you damaged yourself and if anyone else had done the same, no god or bargain would have saved them from my wrath."

He doesn't let me ask any more questions. Those shadowy bonds bind over my mouth in a gag.

He draws me to his mouth again and that ghostly skin disappears. Only his tongue remains and he flicks and fucks me as I squirm at the sensation.

He drives me mad and mindless and I don't need to cross the veil to find my bliss.

And when I come, I pull so tightly against those bonds, I know I'll wear their marks.

They snap as the last waves of my orgasm roll over me and Death draws me back to him, holding me too gently for the violence he just shot through me.

I take a few moments to breathe and let the smells of the incense rising around us seep into my lungs.

"Why do you want me to break our bond?" I ask, tracing the lines of his skull with my fingertips. "We work well together when you're not being an asshole."

"You deserved to live a normal life, Onna. You still do."

"I'm the daughter of a god. My life was never going to be normal."

I kiss the hard line of his jaw, and then slip free of his hold, sliding down the pyre and leaving him to follow me if he chooses.

He does.

17

THE ONCE & NEVER KING

"WE HAVE ANOTHER SOUL TO COLLECT."

Death holds out his hand and I look from him, back to the shimmering Nether I've made no real progress with. He hadn't been lying when he said it would take lifetimes.

This is the furthest he's ventured onto the bridge thus far and I take his offered hand out of habit more than a desire to go back to the mortal realm.

He lifts me to standing, and I let the soul I'd been interrogating slide back into the stream with the other souls.

That smoky cloak falls over me and he hands me the mask as he draws me back toward the sea of candles.

None of them flicker. None of them gutter as they near the end of their wax and the layer of smoke.

"Another deal you've made?" I guess.

"The Easter Bunny has asked for a favour."

The Easter Bunny who has only one devotee…. *Who does the Lady of the Valley wish dead?*

"What *do* you ask for in return for these deals and favours?" He has to need something.

"Nothing."

He doesn't lie to me, but… "Nothing?"

"I don't need anything." His skull tips down and he looks at me with that same blank expression he always wears. "Their payment is unspecified… when I *do* need something in return, I will take it."

"Some day, you're going to want to collect on those favours."

"Perhaps. But not today." As he says it, his domain disappears and the mortal realm forms around us.

A heavy fog clings to the streets. Lamps beside doors act as strange beacons, and I follow Death through tightly packed-in houses. They're crooked stone buildings that seem to support each other, rather than stand on their own. I can't help but wonder if they wouldn't fall down if I pulled at the right brick.

When he stops, it's in front of a squat, single story building with walls so straight, it looks like it was made elsewhere and squeezed in between the crooked edifices around it.

The building is grey, its walls unadorned and its windows covered with dark curtains that barely let slivers of light slip through.

It looks locked up tight, but Death draws us through the closed door as if it isn't there.

Inside…

Boxes are stacked against one wall. Men sit around a table smoking and throwing cards in each other's face as they play some game that involves money changing hands.

There are more empty chairs than there are occupied… as if they're waiting for others who never arrived.

They don't see us, and Death doesn't even spare a glance for them, but I don't follow the line of his sockets just yet.

There are schematics on one wall of what looks like a

water facility, notes scribbled on the paper and a task list marked off. On the other side of the room, a dartboard has a familiar face tacked to it. Her eyes have been cut out and her face is riddled with holes.

The Lady of the Valley may be striking first with this death wish, but it's clear he'd have done the same if he was willing to risk a trip to the old god's realm.

There are plans for most of the city's infrastructure buildings... dates and times scribbled alongside them. Names and numbers.

They have stacks of papers with information on every place people gather in the Valley....

Notes on entry points for the tower. And there's a picture of my sister... though I doubt anyone else would know it's her. The image is grainy, her face digitally smudged, like she was running when they took it.

It would be comical if it wasn't so sinister.

"Gods, what is he planning?" I ask as something dark and ugly slithers along my skin.

"The grasping attempt of a man who once had the Power —diluted though it may have been—attempting to ascend to the top of the tower once more." He looks down at me. "The woman he thought he could cow into submission has taken his place. And when men like Jamus fall, their only goal is to claw their way back to their throne. They don't care how many others they have to shove down and climb over to get there."

I turn to where Death's focus is pinpointed and my gaze falls on a man who would be handsome if not for the sneer that seems etched on his face.

I've met his however many greats-godparent once before and I did not enjoy the experience. Klaus' line was fine to start with, but it quickly soured.

This man is a very distant cousin... though that connection was broken when I bound Death.

Jamus plots and mutters to himself, watching something on a monitor I can't see... but I take a step forward and the motion must draw his attention. He clocks me and his whole expression changes.

I can't feel anything complimentary in the awe on his face. There's something dark and unsavoury that saturates the air here. Something radiating from him.

And then, as if something clears his mind and he finally realises what mask I wear, he stands up, a startled jerk of his whole body and he takes a step back. "How did you get in here?"

The men at the table glance sharply in our direction, but they cast confused looks his way. They don't see me yet.

Death has only shown me to Jamus.

His gaze fixed on me, I know he hasn't seen Death yet, either. But his eyes ghost over me and fix on my mask again.

I wait, watching the emotions roll across his face. Confusion, suspicion... determination.

"You're one of Death's creatures." His eyes flick back and forth, calculating as he studies me. Then, he squares his shoulders. "Bring him to me. I want to make a deal."

"The time for deals is over, Jamus. Your lot has already been cast."

"My *lot*?" He huffs, slapping his hands down on the desk. "How dare you speak to me that way? I am the child of a god!"

"Me too." I say with a laugh. "You're not special."

"What are you then, Death's granddaughter?" He spits the words at me. His sneer is an ugly and twisted thing.

I don't bother correcting him.... Though my mother might scare him more than the god behind me.

His men shift nervously, trying to decide what to do.

"Your time is up. You pissed off the wrong god, and... by the look of things, the Valley will probably be better off without you."

"Better off..." He sputters, pushing away from his desk to stalk around it. "The Valley is *mine.*"

"The Valley belongs to the gods. You weren't doing your job, so they found someone else to do it for you."

"Why do cunts like you always get in my way?" He picks up his gun and I wait. I've been shot before. It's not a pleasant feeling, but it won't kill me, if he even manages to hit me at all.

But the trigger doesn't squeeze, the hammer doesn't drop.

With a frustrated growl, he tosses the gun to the side and drags a knife from the belt of the man beside him.

The blade shatters to dust.

Eyes wide, staring down at the handle of the now useless knife, he finally looks at the men who've gone silent at the table, watching him scream at a phantom.

"Kill her!"

"Kill who?" The one closest asks as he stands. "What's going on?"

It's almost amusing to watch them struggle to make sense of the fit he's throwing.

From behind me, Death sighs. "Toy with him much longer, Onna, and I'll have to give you to the kittens. A cat should be with her kind."

I glance up and over my shoulder at him. "You're not getting rid of me that easily."

I *should* step to the side and let Death touch his scythe to the dead man's skin. But I feel a little vengeful, and... I can draw on Death's power.

The next step I take reveals me to the men who hadn't been able to see me before.

Jamus backs up as I walk him into the wall. He screams for his men to help him and they stand frozen, staring at me… and at Death who follows on my heels.

Those frantic orders die when I catch him around his neck, nails digging into his skin.

"You can't." It's a command and a whimper all at once and I don't have to tell him he's wrong.

He knows.

Grip tightening around his throat, I pull his soul from him and let his body hit the floor.

It's interesting how little difference there is from one soul to another. And yet, he feels unlike any of the others I've sifted from the Nether.

Godkin.

The men who served him stare at me, wide-eyed and with a step back now that they can see me.

I look at each of them in turn. "Don't make me come back for you."

Their murmured responses are the spooked agreement of men too scared to be truthful.

But I've warned them.

What they do now is up to them.

Taking Death's offered hand, I let him drag me back to the old gods' realm.

I know exactly where Jamus' soul belongs.

"I understand now," Death says, releasing my hand, "Why Juun likes you."

"Why doesn't that feel like a compliment."

"She asked if I would let you come play with her."

"And did you tell her no?"

"I told her I don't *let* you do anything." His fingers draw smudged lines down the side of my face. "If you want to torture her devotees with her, you're welcome to it."

I lean into his palm, even though I'm still mad at him. "Even if I wanted to spend more time in Juun's domain, I have too much to do."

His fingers catch in my hair, but he doesn't stop me as I turn to go.

There are souls to save and souls to damn... and torturing the living holds no true appeal.

18

THE HEART OF A DOG

I THROW JAMUS' soul into Suffering and don't look back as I pass under the flow of the souls whose final resting place has yet to be determined.

Death has disappeared again, but the jackal waits for me at the edge of the pit, watching.

"Why did you break the Nether?" Lupu asks, eyes fixed on the doorway to Bliss. "Why not just leave things the way they are?"

I sit on the bridge, perpendicular to them and let my legs dangle over the edge of the pit. "Because Death isn't fair, no matter what he says. He's so focused on equality he forgot there needs to be equity, even in this."

"And you're fair?"

"Not at all." I'm not going to lie to them, or myself. "But there has to be some justice to this. And until I find a better option, I have to do what I think is right."

Lupu studies me for a long moment. "You're very like your mother, you know?"

My mother who won't let Death take children. My mother who can be just as cruel as Juun when she chooses.

132

"Why did you devote yourself to her?" I don't know much about my mother's deals, other than they usually involve the exchange of a piece of the mortal that comes to her. Teeth and other body parts, yes... but also memories and virtues, promises and peace. "What did she take from you while you were still alive?"

"I needed a new heart... she gave me one." Lupu stares at the Nether, the same bitterness in those words seeping into his tone.

"Why does that sound like it came with a trick?"

This time, Lupu's gaze slides to me, irritation in their dark eyes. "Because there are always consequences to *their* deals. She gave me the heart of a dog and even though it shouldn't have worked. It did."

That explains the jackal form. "But... it came with side effects?"

"As you see." They laugh, but it's an ugly sound. "I am more of it and less of myself. Or maybe I was always this way and now others can see it."

"Do you regret it?"

"I don't know."

Lupu takes a deep breath and stares at the Nether they'll never join... at the doorways they'll never pass through.

"I like you." I say. The truth out before I can really consider if it's something they want to hear.

Lupu looks at me askance. "I like you too."

"Will you show me where the Krampus' shrine is?"

"No."

"Then do you want to keep me company as I work my way further down?"

They shrug with one shoulder. "I have nothing better to do."

I count the offshoots as we wind further into the ground.

"Have you been to every one of these?" I ask, ducking into the first tunnel I haven't been in before.

"I think so." They follow, still lagging behind me. "There's not much else to do."

"Two hundred years is a long time to wait around for nothing."

"I haven't had much of a choice."

They follow me into the next tunnel, but the shrine here is completely empty. There's nothing to tell me who it might belong to.

"The forgotten one."

"Who?" I look down at them and they smile up.

"Exactly."

Juun's is full of sand and the souls seem to clump in it, covered in the grit as they roll around and against each other.

"She's cruel to her devotees, even in death." Lupu's tail twitches and they bare their teeth.

"I would expect nothing less."

They start to say something, but their ears twitch, and they turn sharply toward the ceiling.

"He's coming back."

Which means I need to go back up to the Nether.

"Don't let him bully you too much." Lupu says, following me out.

"You might want to tell *me* not to bully him."

We break out of the catacombs as Death steps out of the gauzy shroud.

"Oh, no." Lupu whispers. "He needs to be put in his place."

With one last look toward Death, Lupu disappears back into the catacombs.

"I know what you're searching for, wife. And I know that you'll be disappointed."

"Then tell me where to look now and we can see if you're wrong."

"But, I don't want to disappoint you." He leans close and that transient flesh covers his face a moment before he kisses me. "Perhaps I'm a fool, but I like making you happy."

It's a distraction... but one I'm all too susceptible to.

19

DIRTY DEEDS

IT'S BEEN WEEKS... maybe even months since I've returned to the mortal realm.

I explore the catacombs and sift through the souls in the Nether until Death draws me away. And after he's exhausted me, I sleep like the dead, only to wake with him gone and more souls left to sort.

But today….

I step into the shrine I've been looking for and relief washes over my skin, leaving me numb.

Coloured lights line the ceiling and the smell of cedar hits me in the face like a branch when I cross the threshold.

Souls line the walls trapped in glass boxes wrapped with brightly coloured ribbons and bows. And a pool of them fills the floor in front of an unlit fireplace.

This is where Cassaran should be.

But I don't *feel* him.

Picking up the first box, I open it, but the soul there feels no different than it did when the box was wrapped tight.

"This is why I didn't want you to find the shrine… I told you you would be disappointed."

Death has come to me earlier today and though there is no discernable difference in his bones, I know he's scowling at me.

I ignore that feeling.

It never serves me.

"Where is my brother?"

"He's not here."

"I can see that. Where *is* he?"

Death stays silent.

"I want my brother and I demand that you use one of your stockpiled favours to get him back for me."

"I won't do that."

"Why not?"

He moves as though he's taking a deep breath.

"Will you give me my finger back?" He asks, skull reflecting the swirling pool of souls. "Have you seen enough of the souls I've collected to realise who I am?"

"I've come to realise you're not as bad as you seem to think."

"I am."

"This may be an instance of us having to agree to disagree."

He pauses and for a moment, I wonder if he's given up. But he has not.

"Are you going to make me prove this to you beyond a shadow of a doubt?"

"You can try, but I don't think you'll manage it."

He holds out his hand with the mask.

So, he wants to try now.

I indulge him, slipping the skull mask over my face and taking hold of his still outstretched hand.

He turns me like we're dancing and from one step to the next, we pass between the realms.

It's feels like ages since I've been out of his domain, but... *snow?*

It flutters down from the sky in thick chunks, forming little banks in the courtyard that surrounds the tower.

The familiar chill in the air is like a memory that doesn't touch me.

The sky is dark and the streets are too.

Lamps on iron poles flicker yellow and warm with actual flame and a shop sign creaks in the flurried breeze.

It's a sweets shop that hasn't been open since....

It's not a question of where we are, but, "*When* is this?"

The tower isn't quite as tall as it will be. The lights that glow from its windows are a rich golden colour instead of the vibrant white they were the last time I stepped out into the mortal realm....

A sinking feeling clutches at my stomach.

He wouldn't.

Death doesn't answer me as he slips his arm around my waist and the ground falls away until we are level with the balcony I used to fly little paper birds off of as a child.

This place used to be my home. It's unchanged from the last time I saw it... the last time I dared set foot in it.

And it's Christmas time.

A tree sits in the corner, undecorated and yet, still twinkling with light. And on the couch, elbows on his knees, head bowed, sits my brother.

My brother...

I try to go to him, but Death catches me by the back of the neck like a misbehaving cat.

We are not alone, the three of us.

A large and imposing god stands beside the fireplace, twisting the white hair of his moustache.

I've never seen Klaus in this state, but he's even more vile than the god I've known him as.

"It's about time you showed up," he says, turning to us, and Casaran looks up too… but his eyes pass right by me.

Relief shifts his posture, and I want to shake Death's hold free. I want to go to him, to tell him to stop this, but Death doesn't let me.

"I put this off as long as I could, Onna." Death says to me in a voice so low, I know the others don't hear it. "You've forced my hand."

"He wasn't dead?" Tears prick at the corners of my eyes.

"No… but soon, he will be."

If I hadn't looked for him… Death might have let this night live in a space between time. Casaran wouldn't be looking up at him with *relief.*

It seems Death found the one way he might be able to prove his point.

20

THE POWER & THE PROBLEM

"NOW THAT YOU'VE deigned to show up," Klaus says with a cruelly jolly chuckle. "This mortal has asked for Death and I am willing to make a deal."

"No."

Klaus looks at me as though he's only just seen me. "Is this your bargain to make, godling?"

"This is what I do, Onna." Death says it in my ear, whispered words that make me want to weep. "It doesn't matter who asks, or who they ask for. I come to collect."

"Absolutely not."

I look down at my brother who doesn't recognise me—and why should he? I look nothing like the sister he knew, but he looks exactly the same.

He was older than me, yet still just a boy. Tousled curls covering over his eyes as he looks up at Death and me.

He doesn't speak. He doesn't beg one way or the other.

He just waits.

I don't remember ever seeing him this tired before. But when I lived this timeline, I wasn't here. He ruled the Valley, Ari had given her heart to the god of winter and I… I was a carefree girl roaming the godswood, looking for trouble.

I wasn't here when my big brother needed me... but I'm here now.

"You cannot take him."

"It's already done."

"Is it? You haven't made this deal yet." I wrap my hand around his radius and drag him back to the balcony, pausing only once to look at Klaus. "You'll excuse us."

He watches us with an amusement I don't enjoy, and still... my brother waits. He's accepted his fate, but I won't. He's asked for it, but I won't let him have it.

"Take me back to your realm. We need to negotiate."

We fade between the realms again and I release him when the smoke coils around my knees.

Throwing the mask away, I stalk deeper into his domain, trying to collect my thoughts before I turn and try to throw his head away again.

My frustration leads me all the way back to the Nether.

It isn't split.

The doorways aren't there.

We're still in the past.

And Casaran is still alive. "You didn't take him. All those years ago... you waited until now."

"This should not be a trial for you, Onna." Death's feet scrape across the stone floor, the bones making a hollow sound.

"You knew exactly what you were doing when you took me to him." He knew this was the one thing he could do that would truly hurt me.

"And you knew your brother died. You knew I collected his soul... You've had two hundred years to mourn him. Why is this difficult?"

"You know why." I pace back and forth in front of the Nether.

"Tell me anyway."

"Because I left him to fend for himself when I should have stayed." I stand perfectly still, staring into the Nether and trying not to think about what I'm saying. "Because I couldn't handle the pressure of what he did, and I left him to carry those burdens alone."

I left him when I knew the stress of caring for the Valley was too much. I left him when I knew that doing so would shift that whole burden onto him because I couldn't carry the weight of what staying meant.

"Because people die around me. They always have."

A nanny, three guards, one cook and two grounds keepers. None of them should have died, and yet... they flowed through the Nether in front of me, even now.

"You see connections where none exist. People die, Onna. You couldn't stop it when you were a child, you cannot stop it now. The proximity to you is and has always been purely coincidence."

"But Casaran doesn't have to."

"Onna…" He says my name like he's scolding a child.

But my candle isn't green…. It's burned for far too long. Casaran's didn't burn long enough.

"If I can convince Klaus to change the wording of his bargain…. Will you make your own with me?"

That transient flesh covers over his sockets and his brows pinch with suspicion. "I'm listening."

I play with the cuff around my wrist, twisting his finger and remembering the weight I've got so used to. "Let me decide my brother's fate and I will return the piece of you my mother stole."

Silence stretches between us. He hesitates and I don't know why.

"I'm offering you the one thing you've wanted all this time."

"I accept." His fingers draw along the underside of my jaw and he tips my face up to look at him. "But I have final say over his fate. I may not accept what you decide."

"Then we'll renegotiate."

He dips his head in a nod and releases me. "What do you plan to do with him?"

I don't tell him I haven't figured that out yet. I don't tell him panic has overridden sense. "You'll find out when I'm ready for you to know. Are we at the same point in time... or will Klaus be in his domain?"

Death twirls his finger, and it feels like the world shifts beneath my feet. "It is a day before your brother asks for his bargain... make the most of it."

He offers me the mask once more, but I ignore it, hurrying out of his domain and into Babel.

My haste draws looks from devotees and gods who probably don't know who I am yet. The last time I entered this realm—as far as they're concerned—I was not bound to Death. I was the granddaughter of spring and autumn... not the beautiful corpse so many of them have dubbed me.

Nostalgia tugs at me... the time before my world fell apart.

Too bad I can't appreciate it.

I rush through the people haunting Babel, only stopping when I reach the entrance to the Krampus' domain. The crossed candy cane doorway roils with a feeling as sinister as it is sweet.

Klaus doesn't want visitors. But none of us are going to get what we want from this bargain.

No one but Death.

In the back of my mind, I hear the ticking hands of a clock. Death reminding me he's waiting.

Time doesn't truly matter here… but I've wasted enough of it already.

21

TO EVERYTHING THERE IS A SEASON

KLAUS' domain is… not what I expected.

Unlike his primary, he keeps this place warm, and it smells of spice. But perhaps that is due to the woman sleeping softly in his arms beneath the bower of mistletoe and holly.

In his Krampus form—grey skin and black hair… dark horns and sharp teeth behind lined lips—Klaus is less revolting.

Maybe because this form feels true.

He watches me with a scowl and bared teeth.

"You should not be here, godkin. Go back to your mother or your master. Leave us in peace."

"I can't do that," I say, softly, not wanting to wake the woman who has spent centuries knocking horns with my mother.

But Holly's horns are still attached to her mask, not sprouting from her head.

This is before they are bound.

This is before she's agreed to start the next line that will hold the Power.

Good.

The less certain Krampus is of his relationship, the easier this will be.

The Krampus watches me with his unearthly golden gaze, waiting. He has patience... as far as he knows, he has all the time in the world.

And holding her, he clearly has no intention of moving.

Holly hates my mother, but looks so serene with him. And he, for all his faults, loves her deeply enough I think he'd tear apart both realms to keep her.

Making a deal with my brother that kills him... that's nothing on the balance to a god like him.

"You're going to make a deal with my brother."

"Am I?"

"He has something you need. He's going to ask you for the one thing he can't get himself."

"Is he?"

"He's going to ask you to kill him."

This time, he manages not to come back with a pithy repetition. But I don't give him too long to think up something worse.

"You are going to word the bargain so that you 'give him' to Death. Do you understand me?"

"Why would I do that? Are you here to cut a deal?"

"No. But imagine what your wife will say when I tell her what you've done."

Krampus softens immediately and whispers the word *wife* so low, I see it rather than hear it. He looks down at Holly, still blissfully asleep against him. "She lets me bind her."

"Yes. But I will make sure that doesn't happen if you don't stop my brother from killing himself."

Klaus twists a lock of her hair between his fingers and the golden strands turn green and sparkle like tinsel.

"Will you agree to that?" I ask.

"Threats should put you on my naughty list... but you herald glad tidings..."

I wait, because I can't assume he's agreed.

"It's Christmas time, and you have been nice." Krampus takes a deep breath and his hands tighten on his wife, "I'll give him to Death. Don't you worry."

I turn to go, but hesitate. "If you love her.... Remember she's mortal. We don't always understand the things gods' do. And even if we do... we can't always forgive them."

"Is that advice you should be placing elsewhere, *niece*?"

I look back at him and at her. And then I leave.

He knows he's right. I don't need to tell him.

22

COMPLEX: GOD :: GOD : COMPLEX

DEATH DOESN'T GIVE me a chance to say anything when I return to him. Hand wrapped around mine, he draws me back to the tower and we stand in front of my brother.

Casaran looks up at me and this time he meets my eyes... but still, he doesn't recognise me. There's still no reason for him to.

Klaus on the other hand... he smiles at me like he's got the upper hand. I should be worried, but I have faith that he loves Holly too much to risk what I might do if he crosses me.

When the gods fall in love with mortals, they fall hard.

I wish I knew from experience.

"Welcome back." Klaus waves a gloved hand at me and then looks up at Death, straightening as though he's about to recite a speech.

"I've made a bargain with our dear Casaran. He has given me the last of my mother's Cuckoo clocks and I have promised to 'give him to Death'. What you do with him now is entirely up to you."

Casaran shoots to his feet, spinning so quickly, it knocks

the half empty wine glass from the table. "That wasn't the deal."

There's a frantic terror on my brother's face that I do not like… but I have no choice other than to see this plan through and hope he doesn't hate me for it when it's over.

"That was exactly the deal," Klaus says, drawing the clocks to him and stuffing them in a big velvet sack. He gives me a quick salute before he steps into the fireplace and disappears in a burst of flame.

He vanishes as though he was never here in the first place and we are left to the shadows of those flames.

The room is silent now that he's gone. Casaran stares at the flames, eyes wide and mouth agape.

With a snap of his finger bones, Death douses the flames. The sound snuffs the candles too and we're left in the light of the moon.

"It will help him recognise you," Death says, before he draws his hand down in front of my face.

I feel changed, but I know it's just a trick meant to make things quicker.

Casaran turns to us and he *finally* sees me.

Confusion replaces despair

"What are you doing here, Naya?"

No one's called me that in two hundred years. Not even my mother still uses my full name. But Casaran always used the second half of it. To be funny… to tease me… and then just as a habit.

One he hasn't had centuries to fall out of.

"Did you think I would let you die if I had any other choice?"

He shakes his head and picks up that wine glass, drinking what little remains. "You should be miles away right now."

He drops back to the couch. "You were supposed to be gone. I *sent* you away."

"You sent me away so you could kill yourself...?"

His jaw tenses and then twitches, and he throws the empty glass into the dead fireplace. The glass shatters against the stone.

"I sent you away so she couldn't force you to take my place." He drops his head to his shaking hands. "I can't do this Naya."

"Fine. Don't do this." I hold out my hand and he looks at it like I'm a trick, but after a moments hesitation, he takes it.

His brows pinch as he looks down at my cold skin.

"There are other options."

"I have the Power." He laughs, bitterly. "There are no options."

"I would have found a way."

"You *have* found a way."

"It took me two hundred years."

He stares at me, mouth slack as though he can't decide what to say.

But he doesn't need to say anything.

I feel the illusion Death placed over me fade and know he sees me for what I truly am anymore.

But, I ignore the question in his eyes as I turn back to Death. "Take us to your domain."

Death holds out his hand. "I hope you know what you're doing."

"I do." And I don't.

When Death's bones curl around my skin, we all three slip through the veil between the realms and Casaran shivers as he pulls his hand away, eyes wide as he turns a slow circle and gets his first glimpse of Death's domain.

I'll happily let the oddity of this place distract my brother.

It keeps him from looking at me. He doesn't need to know how hard and fast my heart is fluttering.

All he has to do is refuse what I'm about to offer him and he'll get what he wants…. And I'll lose everything.

"What is going on, Naya? Why are we here, and why do you look like that?"

"I made a deal to save your life."

Casaran lowers his voice… as though Death might not hear him. "Death doesn't make deals with mortals."

"But he has made one with his wife." For however brief a time I can still call myself that.

Casaran's gaze goes to my wrist and his eyes narrow as he looks from Death back to me.

I see the confusion there. I know he's comparing the way Death stands, so far away from me to the way Heim would barely let Ari move a metre from them.

A dissection of the ways in which Death doesn't want me isn't going to help my cause.

"*Because* I have made this deal, your fate is mine to decide. Do you understand?"

He nods and I know he's trying not to actually agree.

"You will die, Casaran. As Death likes to remind me… all mortals do. But you will not die until you have sorted the entirety of the Nether. The souls languishing there require judgement. And you were always good at figuring out who people were."

Casaran's face goes blank. He looks from me to the swirling column, and to Suffering and Bliss beyond it.

"Read their souls, balance their deeds and give them the end they deserve." I take a deep breath, and look at Death. "And then, only when the work is done, *then* you may die."

Casaran wanders, wide-eyed toward the Nether and I let him go.

When he is out of earshot, I ask without looking back, "Is that an acceptable bargain?"

Death trails his knuckles down my neck. "Finish explaining his punishment to him. I will wait for you on my throne."

He leaves us, and Casaran grabs my hand, dragging me closer to the Nether, his eyes always on Death's retreating form.

"Are you okay?"

"I'm better than you were an hour ago."

He looks at me the way he did when we were kids. "That wasn't a yes."

"I've spent the last two centuries thinking you were dead. And then Ari died and mom flipped out. Of course I'm not okay."

"Ari's dead?"

"Not exactly." I take him to the edge of the pit and sit with him, trying to catch him up on two hundred years of history he's missed. "And now… this is your task."

"You're more like the old gods than you know." He shakes his head and looks down at his knees. "You used their wording to trick me into getting something I didn't want."

"Maybe you deserve this as a punishment."

"Maybe I do."

He flinches and I follow his wide-eyed stare to the figure half hidden by shadows.

"And this is Lupu." I say holding my hand out and beckoning the jackal forward. "They are here because of our mother… but I think you'll get along. Lupu, this is my brother, Casaran."

They look him over with sad dark eyes. "He's not in the Krampus' pool after all."

"Not yet." I say, knowing that one day… he'll end up there.

"The Krampus' pool… I don't understand what's going on, Naya."

"Who's Naya?" Lupu drops their head to the side as they sit on their haunches.

"It's her…" Casaran jerks his head at me.

"Onnanaya is my full name, but no one's called me that for centuries."

I twine my fingers with Cas'. "Lupu can show you around and get you up to speed.

"You should have let me go." He says it so quietly, I know he doesn't want me to respond. But I'm not in a mood to give him anything today.

"I mourned you long ago, Cas. I'm not going to do it again."

"What happens now?"

I stand. "You get to work… and I finish my bargain."

Casaran catches my hand and holds me tightly. "I wasn't worth whatever you've had to give him."

"Yes you are."

23

AND THE FINGER TOO

I LINGER CLOSE by as Casaran begins the never-ending process of sorting through the dead.

Lupu sits at the edge of the pit and I have no idea what they talk about, but when I see my brother laugh for the first time in centuries... I know it's finally time to let him go.

The cuff around my wrist grew tighter and heavier as the hours passed.

I don't say goodbye.

Even if Death is no longer bound to me, there is nothing that will bar me from coming back to visit. I will simply need a mask again. And I have no intention of leaving any of them alone.

I follow a path preset by the candles, a dark line in the smoke that leads me back to Death.

He waits elbow on his throne, skull resting in his hand. A flicker of that transient flesh makes me wonder if he's scowling at me... but it's gone before I could truly venture a guess.

"The mask?" I ask, holding out my hand, keeping the wrist with his finger, firmly at my side.

But Death picks me up drawing me to him with those invisible strings, and I hold my breath when his fingers wrap around me holding me like a doll once more.

He draws his thumb over my forehead and the mask forms, falling over my face like it's bone moulded to my flesh.

"A deal's a deal." I offer him my wrist and stare at his dark sockets as he wraps his hand around my arm… lining up the end of the missing finger to the metacarpal it was attached to before my mother stole it.

A hollow ache stabs through me before he's even removed his hand, and I take some small solace in the fact that he flinches too… as if it hurts him as well.

"As agreed," I say, my voice sounding weaker than I remember it. "I release you from your bond and return what was stolen."

He draws his hand away slowly, opening and closing it as if he's never used it before. I clench my jaw so hard it aches. The pain only mirrors what's burrowed deep inside me.

I'd forgotten that the bond was more than just wearing him on my skin. It had burrowed deep into my veins and filled my bones.

The loss leaves me hollow and I grip his arm to keep myself from pitching forward at the lightheadedness that washes over me.

"Are you happy?" The question slips out before I can decide if I truly want the answer.

"I got what I wanted."

It's not a yes… but I don't know if Death's ever been happy.

Maybe he doesn't have that power.

"Can I have one more kiss before I go?" I ask. I won't

call it a last kiss. I'm not giving him up simply because he's not mine anymore.

Mortal as I am, that should be all that I want.

It's all that I can ask for.

And it's all that he gives me.

His fingers hold my face steady and his lips coast over mine.

I can't take anything more than he offers. He isn't mine anymore.

The mask hides the tear that slips free.

And when he releases me, I leave in silence. I won't let him hear my voice shake.

I follow the tunnel up and out through my tomb. The mausoleum is cold and I don't look at any of the empty promises there.

The mortal world feels just as hollow as I do.

Outside, the wind is fuzzy on my skin, the fading light of dusk leeches the colour from the Valley, and my energy seems to slip from me with every step.

I wander through the city, barely noticing those around me, and I cross the field, only vaguely aware of the bugs coming out to sing in twilight.

Opening the gate to Ari's home is harder than I remember, the hinges creaking the way my joints feel like they should.

Ari sits on the same bench, humming the same tune she always did. Head tipped back, resting on the wood with its chipped blue paint, she looks as cold as I feel.

"You look happy."

When she opens her eyes, they go wide, and she stares at me for a moment before she says, "You gave it back."

"I did."

"It's strange that I'd forgotten how much the binding changed you."

"You're one to talk, ice queen."

She chuckles, but her smile is forced. "You sound tired."

"I am."

She catches my hand in hers and her brows pinch as she looks at them "The room is yours, as it always is."

"Thank you... I just need to lie down for a while."

She nods and lets me go. She doesn't voice the concern I see in her eyes, and I don't offer her anything more than what I've already given her, simply by coming back here.

The house is warm and the air prickles at my skin and when the door closes me into the small room Ari has always set aside for me, I take a moment to catch my breath... hating that the world effects me this way again.

I don't look at myself in the mirror. I don't know the person I am and I don't want to.

She was a child and now she's an old woman... nothing that happened in between makes sense on her skin.

I crawl into bed, feeling—for the first time in a long time—unwell.

24

PLAYING CATCH-UP

THE MOON FLICKERS behind gauzy curtains when I wake. My mind and body are at odds and it *feels* like I'm being watched. But the shadows in the corner are just shadows.

Death is done with me and I don't expect to see him any time soon… not unless I chase him down in his domain.

But sleep eludes me and I finally give up after the clock has clicked past two more hours into the morning.

I'm restless even though I feel the keen fingers of exhaustion trying to drag me back to bed, just to stare at the ceiling.

There's no point waiting around for the day to start, so I don't. I flick on the light as I get dressed and flinch away from my reflection….

I'm older than I thought I was.

Perhaps my candle, free to burn again, is playing catch-up.

Perhaps I've forgotten too much of my previous self.

Slipping out of the house, I'm as quiet as I can be, to not wake Ari.

She'd want to come with me… to help. But my thoughts aren't fit for company.

The city is asleep as I find my way back onto the cobbled steps.

Where I'm going... I don't know, but I've done this hundreds of times before—wandered the city until my feet take me somewhere I need to go.

Except... I don't feel the dying anymore. There's no one calling to me through the veil... no one tugging on Death's power to get to me.

And when the shadows shift, it's two mortal men that step out into the street in front of me... not Death.

"Not safe to be wandrin' the streets alone at night, little lady." The affectation of his voice is so fake, I might have laughed, but I can't be bothered.

I don't even bother to catalogue their features before trying to move around them.

They don't let me.

"It's safe enough if you get out of my way."

The first looks at the second who takes a long drag off a cigarette and then flicks it away. "We're just trying to be nice and she jumps straight to rude. That's not very neighbourly."

"And you are in our neighbourhood. Seems only right that you should be cordial."

I blink at him for a moment, trying to decide if I'm in the right point in time.... Or if I've somehow fallen backward in it again.

But there's nothing else about the tableau that feels like this is the past.

"Come on," the smoker says, knocking the other's shoulder. "She doesn't look like she's going to be any fun."

"She can be as much fun as we make her."

"Gods, you're so boring."

I say it before I remember I'm not bulletproof anymore.

I probably *should* be afraid of them, but I can't find the energy, even for that.

"Boring?" The smaller of the two straightens, glaring at me. "You look like you should be old enough to know better."

He takes a step toward me, but he doesn't take another.

Both of them make strangled sounds and then collapse, their skulls knocking against the cobbles with a dull thud.

Death looms like a shadow above them, but I can't see their souls.

Even still... I'm certain no one asked for their deaths. And the both of them having heart attacks at the same time....

"What happened to your rules?"

"What happened to not wanting to die?" Death steps over them and looks down at me. "You are mortal again, Onna. You need to start acting like it."

"And you're not bound to me anymore... *when* I die shouldn't matter. But I could have dealt with those two on my own."

"Could you?" He pushes me and I fall back, stumbling. He catches me a moment before I'd hit the ground. "Somehow I don't think you could deal with anyone on your own."

"You wanted to be rid of me... so why are you still here?"

"I never said that." But he fades into the night again... disappearing like a coward and I leave the bodies where they lie.

There are dozens of entrances to the godswood from the edges of the city and I slip down one of the paths I've travelled most.

The ground is clear. Wide flat stones cover most of it. There are few roots in my way. And even though the sky has barely begun to lighten, I'm not worried about falling or losing my way.

But each step makes me look over my shoulder, I expect to see him following me—I'm hoping for it

Except, I need the space.

I need some peace and quiet and to clear my head.

But the further I walk and the brighter it gets, the warmer the air feels in my lungs... the more my skin buzzes and prickles.

I'd forgotten the way that exertion played with my senses.

My ears begin to thrum and my eyes water as I climb the godswood path up the side of the Valley.

There's a pond nearby and I go to it, pausing every few steps to catch my breath.

The bench I remembered is gone. Splintered by malicious hands, not weather or wear. I look at the remains and my hips start to ache as my stillness gives me nothing to distract myself from the pain that had slowly built from nothing.

That crystal clear pond reflects a woman I don't know back at me.

One look is all I need... my life is definitely catching up to me.

I sit in the clover, heart and lungs begging for relief.

I'll just rest for a moment.

But when the flowers tickle at my arms and the moss kisses my face, I know... I'm not getting back up.

25

A TIME TO DIE

AN INSECT BUZZES past my face and I flinch away from it. Startling awake as the warm sunlight filters down through the trees and glints off the pond.

But I'm not alone.

Others might think that Death was out of place here as he looks down at me with his expressionless face.

But he is at home here as he is anywhere else. Grass and flowers poke through his ribcage and it makes me sad that they don't tickle him.

"I don't think you've ever frowned when you've woken to find me."

"I didn't think it would be my turn this soon…" I haven't even had a chance to convince him he liked having me around.

"It's not. Not quite yet."

"Death doesn't intervene."

"Death doesn't fall in love."

"No. He doesn't." I reach up and trace my fingers down the length of his jaw. "Can I have one last kiss… before you take me?"

Those pale blue, translucent lips form over his teeth and he's scowling too.

"No kiss will ever be a last kiss for you, Onna." But he clamps his hand around my wrist and gives me what I ask for.

That strange and familiar sensation flutters over my skin and we fall through the forest floor out of the mortal realm and onto that bed I'd barely got used to thinking of as my own, its dark velvet curtains closing us in.

And I flinch back from him. I'm not wearing a mask. By rights I should have turned into a horrible creature already, but, "I rebind myself to you. Never to take myself from you again. I am yours Onna... and I would be very happy if you would be mine."

Our fingers scrape together as he twines our hands together and holds them up for me to see.

His finger is back around my... wrist?

"It's back where it belongs."

Except my arm is all bone now too.

My left hand and arm are black bone, no flesh left behind.

I'm not a skeleton like him... not completely. Most of me is still here.

"Why do you want me to live forever?"

"Why would I want you to die?"

Fire burns in his sockets, bright and warm.

"All mortals have to die."

"Not you." He kisses me and I shiver as his body covers over mine.

"I considered a world without you in it... and I refuse to let it exist." He's smaller now, or maybe I'm larger, but our bodies fit together more easily. "I love you, Onna. I'm not supposed to, but how could I not?"

His hand travels down my side and my clothes disappear, leaving nothing between us but more unspoken words.

"I loved you before I was this woman." I take a deep breath and my breasts scrape across his ribs. "I loved you when I hated you and I loved you when I couldn't stand to look at you. I never wanted to break our bond, because I could imagine you returning that love."

"Your tenacity is one of the reasons I love you. Never lose that."

"I'm glad my mother forced this bond the first time." I draw him down to me and whisper my next words against his phantom lips. "I was yours... long before you were mine."

"Will you let me love you the way you deserve?"

I know it's folly to give a god tacit permission, but.... "You may love me any way you see fit."

"Good." He rolls over me, pinning me down.

I gasp—grateful that my lungs have lost their burn—and I tease him. "I'm actually old now... be careful you don't break a hip."

He chuckles and his lips coast down my chest to my stomach. As he goes, a mirror forms out of the smoke on the ceiling and I'm not old anymore... because I'm not the version of the woman I was born as... I'm his wife again. The face I've grown used to, the white hair I have not....

Except that my left arm is nothing but black bone... and the left half of my face as well.

Like the pieces of my effigy that crumbled away.

I have been changed and marked by Death so many times... but this time, it's for keeps.

His tongue covers me and I flinch back from the sensation, a memory fluttering through my mind.

"You told me once, that you could make me come simply by snapping your fingers."

"I believe I used it as a threat."

"Show me."

He chuckles as he lowers his head to my pussy once more. "Always in such a rush."

But he raises his hand and with a sharp snap of his fingers….

The sound ripples through me and the orgasm that trails it drives the air from my lungs and bows my back. I shake as all my muscles tense and it rips through me, wave after wave until it finally slows and dies.

"Curiosity sated?" He asks.

All I can do is nod and reach for him.

My god comes to me and when I sling one leg over his pelvis, he slides his phantom cock along my wet pussy.

His party trick certainly has me ready for anything.

I hold him inside me, keeping him there, in me and on me. "You said you're always with me."

"Yes."

"Did that change when you had your finger back?"

"No." His three remaining fingers drag over the bony side of my face. "I have been with you since the day we met. And I will be with you until you choose to be free of me… with no bargain's influence."

"Good. Because we have centuries to make up for."

"I am yours, Onna. I love you and I will be yours until the world ends and is remade."

EPILOGUE - THE AFTERLIFE AS WE KNOW IT

CASARAN TAKES the soul I hand him with a grimace. Whether it's for my skinless hand or the deeds he can feel in the man's soul... I don't know.

I don't ask.

"Have you told Ari?" He asks as he turns the glare onto the soul in his hand.

"Yes." She also knows the details of my... transformation. Keeping Casaran from her felt like an unnecessary cruelty. "She's glad you're not dead."

"But she can't visit me."

"Too many gods feel they are owed her life. And even if I can stop that from happening.... The ones who won't get their way would probably torture her just for the fun of it." Death can't intervene in the other gods' business.

He nods and turns the soul over in his hands once more.

"Do you want to let mom—our grandparents—know you're not actually dead?"

"I think Ari's enough for now. If you tell mom, she's going to come down here and scream at me and as for Ester and Gren…. They don't need to know. All it will do is give them something else to scheme about."

"Our family is overrun with secrets."

I certainly haven't told him most of mine. I won't ask for any more of his, and we should both leave Ari well alone.

"And I learn more by the day." His nose wrinkles and a moment later he throws the soul through the veil into Suffering. "I sometimes think this life you gave me is a punishment."

I don't deny it. I won't lie to him.

He snorts at me and shoos me away, grabbing another soul from the streaming Nether.

Casaran may not enjoy the dead… but he would have been among them otherwise. It's not a punishment I feel particularly guilty for inflicting.

But what I want to do next is a reward.

Death stands in the middle of his sea of candles, looking down at them like a gardener inspecting a bed of flowers.

"Do you see them?" I ask, stopping beside him and looking at the bobbing flames. "When you look at the candles do you actually see the people in the mortal realm living out their lives? Or are they just candles to you?"

"I see what I want to see." Her reaches down and lifts my chin with a single finger. "And right now, I see a woman who has a request."

He always knows. *Silly god.*

"I do. And I see a god who is going to give me what I want."

"Within reason."

"And without." I chew on my lip, but he doesn't ask me what I want, he likes making me be the one to ask. "I want you to release the jackal from their service to you."

His thumb stills beneath my chin. "I can't."

"You can."

"They stay here as they are, or they die. Those are the only two options."

"You should know you can't lie to me."

"It's not a lie."

"It's not the truth." That phantom flesh shows confusion on his brow. "Give them to me. That is in your power."

"If you want a pet…" He takes my hand and presses my knuckles to his teeth. "The jackal is in your keeping until you choose to relinquish them."

"Lupu?" I say their name, knowing they'll hear me and they appear through the veil that separates the living's candles from the Nether.

And they stop, immediately after, their tail twitching warily, tucked between their legs.

They always keep out of reach of Death, so scared of him without needing to be.

"Do you want to die again?" I ask, drawing their attention back to me.

"No."

"You shouldn't have to."

Their eyes narrow at me and then flick from Death back to me again. "Are you breaking the rules again?"

"Always."

I pull away the sliver of bone that I broke from my radius by accident days ago, shivering as it scrapes free.

"What is that?" Lupu watches my hand with suspicion creasing their brow, but they creep closer.

"It's your freedom. Do you want it?"

Lupu looks at Death again and then at me and dips their head in a sharp nod. "I trust you."

"Good. This might hurt."

Their eyes widen and I slam my hand against their chest, burying the splinter of my bone into their dog's heart.

Eyes flashing through every possible colour of fire, Lupu backs away from me, shaking as their fur turns black with a shiver of their skin and their teeth fall out, regrowing gold.

When they look up at me, the fire that didn't burn above their head now flickers from their eyes.

"You are a hellhound now. You are technically my servant, but I hold you to no service. You may leave this domain and this realm as you choose... within limits."

"What limits?"

"Hunt down a Yule Lad in the depths of Heim's domain. They will tell you what you are and how to be."

Once more, Lupu looks at Death and back to me. With a nod of their darkly maned head they lop away... hopefully to find what they couldn't have before.

"You," Death says, taking my hand and drawing me up to hold me against his ribs. "Know far too much about the way this realm works."

"It's our realm... and I've had plenty of time to learn its secrets." I press my lips to his jaw. "Time a certain god could have spent distracting me if he hadn't been so set on making me die."

"I never wanted you to die... I only wanted you to live."

"We can do more than enough of that now."

ABOUT DALIA

Dalia Davies came up with the title for "Railed by the Easter Bunny" as a joke. But that joke grew legs and hopped right out of her brain and onto the page for you to read and enjoy with her. She writes fantasy romance that pairs old gods and monsters with mortal women who get exactly what they want and maybe a little more than they came for. Living in the southwestern US, she's let the outside heat permeate her stories and hopes they leave you panting.

Find more info and sign up for the newsletter at www. daliadavies.com

Become a Patron

For early access, exclusive stories, sneak peeks at art, and book mail, at patreon.com/daliadavies

MORE BOOKS BY DALIA DAVIES

Valley of the Old Gods

Railed by the Easter Bunny

Banging the Easter Bunny

Railed by the Krampus

Railed at the Bacchanal

Railed by the Reaper

Railed by the Tooth Fairy

Railed by the Yule Cat

Railed by the Leprechaun

Shadow Zone Brotherhood

Richter Scale

Seismic Drift

Trench Tactics

The Devil's Dance

The Dame & The Devil

The Flame & The Fallen

The Halo & The Heathen

Stand-Alone Titles

The Two Queens of Firixina

Velvet Steel

Coven of Curiosities

Blue Moon Mistress

Vanquishing

Love's First Bite

CONTEMPORARY ROMANCE AS ANDI SIMMS

A Taste of Something Wicked

Fate at Fault

Fair Bargain

With This Vow

All Fun & Games

At Summer's End

Like & Sub

Nine Two Five

Gifted & Talented

A Taste of Something Wicked Print Omnibus Vol 1

A Taste of Something Wicked Print Omnibus Vol 2

DETAILED CONTENT WARNINGS

Mentions of: Blackmail, Femicide, Suicide

Blackmail: In Last Meal (CH7) Onna and Death go to collect on a death deal and the should they collect belongs to a loanshark/blackmailer.

Femicide: In Funeral Rites & Wrongs (CH12), Onna and Death go to collect on a death deal where a man has asked for the death of a woman who rejected him. Certain language in this chapter may be abrasive.

Suicide: Onna's brother's suicide is mentioned throughout the book and is one of her main motivators. It is not shown on page, but is referenced heavily.

Torture

In Cruel Cruel Summer (CH15) Onna goes to Juun's domain to punish the man who made a bargain for a woman's death (see Femicide above). Juun is shown torturing men who have come to her for bargains. Her throne is made of naked men bound in barbed wire, she stabs one of them through the hand with a knife-stiletto, and other "devotees" are in various states of pain.

Onna uses Death's power to torture the man who killed Rilla by tightening the concertina wire holding him to a post in the middle of Juun's desert.

SPICE MENU

A frustrated Onna fucks herself on Death's finger - Ch 4 "Death's Kiss"

Death tongue fucks Onna - Ch 6 "Amore Aeternus"

Death fucks Onna with his phantom cock (FINALLY) - Ch 8 "A Little Death"

Onna pulls a pseudo Mary Shelley and fucks death on her tomb (wax play) - Ch 10 "Boned"

Death sits her in the palm of his hand and eats her out like she's a jelly donut. - Ch 16 "Heads will Roll"

Death makes her come with a snap of his fingers and then makes her come some more. - Ch 25 "A Time to Die"

Made in the USA
Las Vegas, NV
28 November 2024

12180571R10105